FIRST AID

Janet Davey is the author of four novels: *English Correspondence*, longlisted for the 2002 Orange Prize, *The Taxi Queue* and *By Battersea Bridge*. She lives in London.

ALSO BY JANET DAVEY

English Correspondence
The Taxi Queue
By Battersea Bridge

JANET DAVEY

First Aid

VINTAGE BOOKS
London

Published by Vintage 2005

2 4 6 8 10 9 7 5 3

Copyright © Janet Davey 2004

Janet Davey has asserted her right under the Copyright, Designs
and Patents Act 1988 to be identified as the author of this work

First published in Great Britain in 2004 by
Chatto & Windus

Vintage
Random House, 20 Vauxhall Bridge Road,
London SW1V 2SA

www.vintage-books.co.uk

Addresses for companies within The Random House Group Limited
can be found at: www.randomhouse.co.uk/offices.htm

The Random House Group Limited Reg. No. 954009

A CIP catalogue record for this book
is available from the British Library

ISBN 9780099469643

The Random House Group Limited supports The Forest
Stewardship Council® (FSC®), the leading international forest
certification organisation. Our books carrying the FSC label are
printed on FSC®-certified paper. FSC is the only forest certification
scheme endorsed by the leading environmental organisations,
including Greenpeace. Our paper procurement policy can
be found at: www.randomhouse.co.uk/environment

Printed in Great Britain by Clays Ltd, St Ives plc

Friday

1

If you want to know how things used to be and still are, you can go on a train to the far end of the East Kent line and start paying attention after Ashford International. The train itself is suited to nostalgia: no automatic doors or high-tech hums, just doors that slam and windows that open wide enough to lean out of, and which have to be leant out of, in order to open the doors from the outside. Then there are the stations, neat but run-down, built like houses, with windows and chimneys and iron railings. And nothing is spoiled by getting out. It is worth getting out and looking up and down the straight tracks, blurred by the seed heads on the grasses. Check the times of the return trains, two an hour, in the still, square station hall and set off. You will have to ignore the cars, parked and moving, bright and insignificant against the tall old houses, ludicrously capacious against the low terraced cottages. This is routine obliteration and you'll soon come to the street with the shops. Everyone likes old shops: yellow cellophane stretched across windows to keep out the sun, items of household linen you haven't seen for years, roller towels, kettle holders, floor cloths, piles of tea cloths for eternal washing up. And in the junk shop, the remains of the remains of people's lives. Always more saucers than cups. There's a sense of loss, but offhand, not profound. Catch the rapid speech and abrupt applause of midday radio comedy, coming from the back.

The train home, in the late afternoon, is slightly busier, but you still have a compartment to yourself. The front carriage is out in the sun and the rest of the train is shaded by the scalloped edges of the station roof. The other people getting on are mostly local – going a few stops at the end of the working day or travelling up for an evening in London. Already the capital overflows to meet you, seeping down the line. Loose pages from the *Evening Standard* flutter on the seat. The last of the sea breezes.

You hear footsteps, voices and a scuffle outside. The whistle blows. The door of the next compartment is opened. There is a thud and something heavy scrapes along the floor.

'Don't just stand there, Ella. Help, for God's sake. I can't get this lot on with you in the way. The train's about to leave.'

It is a woman speaking – the open-air sound of someone saying goodbye – though the words aren't goodbye.

'Let it leave.'

'Well, carry something, or pick up your sister.'

A boy appears in the gap that runs down the middle of the carriage. He's wearing a baggy T-shirt and jeans and heavy trainers. He looks tall enough to be twelve or thirteen but his face has a child's roundness.

'There's more space here, Mum,' he says.

'Ella, move some of this stuff. I won't be able to shut the door. Sorry, was that your foot? Sorry. Ella, pick Annie up so I can get these bags in.'

The boy turns and tugs at a suitcase that has appeared behind him.

'Ella, push that through. Help, for God's sake.' The woman's voice is inside now.

The suitcase lurches through the gap that connects the compartments and bangs against the boy's shins.

'She didn't say kick it,' he says.

The door slams and the train moves off, rattling out of the station. The boy braces one foot against the seat and heaves the case on to the luggage rack. His arms shake with the effort, but he wedges it in place. He goes back to the gap and gathers up a battered holdall and a plastic laundry bag with its handles tied together. He swings them both up and presses them into the remaining space.

The woman appears, but she doesn't settle. She pushes strands of hair away from her face. Her attention shifts from object to object, then, distractedly, back down the carriage. A little girl trails behind her. She clasps a piece of her mother's skirt and with the other hand pulls at one of the straps of her sun-dress, hitching it back on her shoulder.

'Rob, we'll never get it all down again,' the woman says.

'It's out of the way, isn't it? Stop fussing, Mum. Give me what you've got in your hands,' the boy says.

He snatches two bulging black bin liners, tied into knots at the top, and tries to fit them on to the opposite rack.

'Where's the buggy?' she says.

'I haven't seen it,' he says, still occupied with the bags.

'I didn't leave it on the platform, did I?'

An older girl pushes past her. She ignores everyone present and walks with exaggerated carefulness round a squashed chip on the floor. Then she examines a spare stretch of seat. She stares at the black disc of flattened chewing gum that is on the upholstery and sits clear of it. It is impossible not to watch her. She wants to be watched while pretending that no one is there to do the watching. She is a year or so older than the boy. Otherwise she looks like her mother. They have the same facial bones and almost identical hair. She pulls a magazine out of her bag, opens it across her knees, and flicks through the pages.

The woman moves back to the other compartment and the little girl goes after her, trying to catch at her hand.

'No, there it is,' she says. 'Sorry, was that your foot? Sorry. Annie, don't walk that way. We're sitting here. Careful. Mind that umbrella. No, don't cry. You didn't hurt yourself. Get up, Annie. We're on the train.'

3

The woman returns, drops the folded buggy on the floor and sits down. She leans her head back, exhausted. The little girl picks herself up, examines her knees, then licks a finger and tries to rub the dirty marks off.

'Leave it where it is, Rob, there's enough up there,' the woman says through closed eyes.

The boy gets hold of the buggy and grapples with it above his head until it is clamped in place. The woman glances up and shuts her eyes again.

The train runs close to the cliff edge, in and out of tunnels stamped into the chalk. You can see a ferry in the Channel, people walking their dogs. It's not much of a sea view, but it is the sea. No one else looks out of the window.

'Mum, that's disgusting. Annie's eating stuff off the floor,' says the boy.

The woman reaches forward and pulls the little girl to her. She half pinches her cheeks and fishes out the chip. The child's eyes light up in astonishment before scrunching up. She begins to cry.

'Shut up, Annie,' says the boy. 'Do you want a drink?'

'What did you say that for?' says the woman. 'There isn't a drink.'

'There is,' says the boy. 'It's in one of those bags.'

'Oh my God,' says the girl.

'I'll get it,' says the boy. 'Shut up, Annie.'

He climbs on to the seat and pulls down the laundry bag.

'It's not in there,' says the woman. 'Please don't do this, Rob.'

'I know where it is, Mum. I can get at it when I've moved some of the stuff down.'

He stretches up and roots about, destabilising the pile and nearly toppling it to the floor. Eventually he hands down a small carton. The woman takes it and gives it to the child.

'Get down now, Rob.'

'I've just got to put it all back properly.'

4

A ticket collector comes through the door, which connects with the driver's cabin.

'Get off of them seats.'

The boy tries to push the bags back into place.

'I said off. People got to sit on them.'

The man stands and waits while the boy gives one last shove and clambers down. He looks at the woman. Down her right cheek, from the corner of her eye to the edge of her jaw, is a stripe of purple skin broken by a series of pale horizontal strips of sticking plaster that interlock like a large zip fastener. The child is sitting at her feet, trying to fit a straw into a carton. Orange liquid wells up and drips down her leg.

'Don't let me catch you doing that again,' the ticket collector says to the boy. He turns to go.

'This is sick,' says the girl, without raising her eyes.

'Sorry?' The ticket collector looks back over his shoulder.

'This magazine. It's sick. I found it on the train. You should clear up. Not leave this kind of stuff lying around,' she says.

'Shut up, El,' says the boy.

'You shut up. And don't call me El.'

'Nothing to do with me,' says the ticket collector. He disappears.

'What did you say that for?' the boy says.

'What do you mean?' the girl says.

'About picking it up on the train. You didn't.'

'I know. It's yours. I found it at home. It's sick. Games about total annihilation and hamster firing squads. You give them marks out of ten. You'll be into cake decoration next. Death Row in different-coloured icing. Haven't you got anything better to do?'

'Leave him alone, Ella. He's not hurting you,' the woman says.

'Not hurting me. Is that all you care about? Just because you've been hurt you don't have to take it out on the rest of us. Look at him. Ticking things in catalogues and fitting the fucking bags on the rack like Lego. I've got to share a room with him at Gran's.'

The girl starts to pluck at the bead bracelet round her wrist, twanging the elastic.

'Annie'll whinge all the time. And you'll hang about like a ghost, not telling us what's going on. And Gran and Grandad'll be fussing round and making hot drinks and locking up at ten o'clock. Locking up. That'll be about it, won't it? All banged up together. What are we going away for, anyway?' she says.

The train jolts and stops. The engine chatters for a minute. Then cuts out. There is silence. Outside are fields and hedges and, in the distance, orderly rows of houses. The sea has gone.

The girl looks away from her mother and down the length of the carriage. Suddenly she grabs her bag, reaches the door, pulls the window down and leans out. She opens the door and jumps.

'Mum,' says the boy. He is kneeling up on the seat, staring out.

The engine starts into life.

'Mum. What are you going to do?'

'Shut the door, Rob, before Annie falls out.'

The boy looks at her, agonised. The train begins to move. He gets up, rests one hand on the door-jamb and slams it shut with the other. The train picks up speed.

'What you up to now?' The ticket collector is standing there again. 'What you doing with the window wide open?'

'Nothing.'

The boy turns round, keeping his back to the door and hiding the view. The man looks sharply at him.

'Were you smoking? It's the same, you know, out the window or in. Counts the same. Hundred pound fine.'

He approaches the boy and sniffs.

'Shut the window, then. You can't leave it like that.'

The boy turns back and slowly shuts the window all the way. The temperature rises as soon as it is fully closed. The ticket collector looks round the compartment.

'I thought there were two of you kids.'

'There are,' says the woman.

'No. Two big 'uns, I mean. I see the little 'un.'

'No,' says the woman.

He looks at her, but her eyes register nothing. He shrugs. The little girl tugs at her mother's hand.

'Doesn't she talk?' he asks.

'She's tired,' says the woman. 'Once she starts, she doesn't stop.'

'Where's your sister?' he says, bending over. 'Has she left you?'

The child climbs on her mother's lap, puts in her thumb and stares at him over her curled-up hand. The man straightens up.

'Let's see your tickets, then.'

The boy fumbles in his back pocket and hands over the tickets to be clipped. He watches as the ticket collector clips yours. A piece of thistledown that has blown in through an open window further down the train floats past. The little girl follows it with her eyes and just as it comes within reach she takes out her thumb and grasps it. She holds it in her cupped hands and looks at it. Then she puts it in her pocket and snuggles back into her mother's lap. The ticket collector moves off down the carriage.

'Mum, I asked you,' the boy says.

The woman strokes the child's hair with slow, regular movements.

'Mum, what are you going to do?' the boy says.

'Nothing.'

'You can't just do nothing.'

'She wasn't hurt, was she? You saw her pick herself up?' He nods.

'Leave it. She'll be all right,' the woman says.

'But, Mum. You should tell someone.'

'Who?'

'I don't know. The police. Someone at the next station.'

'It wouldn't do any good.'

'You can't say that.'

'Let's get where we're going. Leave it.'

'Mu-um.' The word collapses into two parts like the trite ending to a song.

The child looks at you. You don't react. Smiling at her wouldn't be right, sentimental complicity. She wouldn't have smiled back.

2

Jo closed her eyes again. She knew who was there. Annie and Rob. No other members of the family now. And a stranger, sitting in the corner seat, with her back to the engine. Most people prefer to face the way the train is going, though in a crash they are better off the other way round and she might have taken that into account. It wasn't an entirely stupid decision. There were more accidents on the railway than there used to be. Jo could feel the woman looking at her. She had looked several times already, and now she could do it thoroughly. The view under Jo's eyelids was restless and blotchy, not peaceful. She wished it would settle down. With the movement of the train her vision wavered – near, then receding – an indeterminate red. She could have done with her being human, the stranger. She tried to remember what she looked like. There was only redness now where she used to see – redness with wisps and filaments hatching and dispersing. She wanted to think of safe, material things. It would calm her. For a moment her mind's focus shifted. She imagined Ella scrabbling up an embankment, running over fields, growing smaller and smaller as the distance claimed her – then just redness.

Annie stretched up to her and pulled at the flesh of her arm, as if it were cloth in a sleeve. The action seemed experimental, not demanding. Jo went back to stroking the child's head. This seemed to soothe her and was less trouble than lifting her back on the seat. She thought, it's no good

9

bothering about what other people think. They can think what they like. But she couldn't stop whatever came before bothering; the consciousness of the other person seeing and judging. The train was slowing down. Signals again. It was quiet outside. The instinct to open her eyes and check where they were had gone, but her thoughts steadied with the stopping of the train. She knew approximately where Ella had jumped off and, with less certainty, where they were now. She had never been to either place.

No one goes to the strips of land bordering the line between stations, unless their house and garden back onto them, and there were no houses. People don't clamber over a field to watch the trains as they used to, taking their children to wave. Jo had a picture in her mind of her mother waving. A girl with dark bobbed hair leaning over a fence. It was like a photograph, though no such photograph existed. Even after the steam trains had finished, the waving carried on. Habits endure for a while and then stop. Now kids chuck stones, or worse, at the railway lines; mess up the system and everyone's mornings or evenings. We apologise for the late running of such and such a train, they say, due to an incident. By then, the kids who did it are in school, or having their tea. We are sorry for the inconvenience caused.

Jo knew what she would have seen through the windows. She had often done the journey. On her own, or with her children – to visit the grandparents. Never with Peter. Journeys with her ex-husband involved a car. She and the children changed trains at London Bridge – up the stairs and over the footbridge to the other platform. Someone always wanted a drink. Someone always wanted the toilet. It seemed to her hopeless that she was still occupied with these wants. Other things came to an end. But children's demands continued.

She felt, as she always felt, that, having left the seaside towns behind, she was already at her destination. The territory behind the sea margin was hardly different from the edges of London. Brick terraced housing and in-filling from the first seven decades of the twentieth century – not the best samples. Streets that became their own likenesses when you turned the corner. No vistas. The pub isolated on a roundabout, the newsagent, the bookies and the take-away squashed up snugly together. The scene was similar to what greeted them when they left the station at the London end and walked to her grandparents' house in East Greenwich – an unmodernised district tucked in between old Thames wharves and the Blackwall Tunnel Southern Approach Road.

The Garden of England, they used to call it, her grandfather said, when Jo said she and Peter were moving to Kent. I don't know if you'd agree with that. What do you want to go and live there for, her grandmother said, aren't the jobs in London good enough for him?

Jo's former house, the one that had had to be sold when her husband left, had been cheerful-looking – flat-fronted, painted blue, with pretty railings that were rusty but more or less intact, only a few curlicues missing. Leaning out of the back bedroom window, she had been able to see the sea. She still missed waking up there. She wished that she and the children had been able to stay put but they hadn't been able to afford that. They had lost continuity. She had done what she could to keep ordinary family life going, but Ella and Rob had known the difference between a solid house and a sheet draped over a clotheshorse. Ella's carefully kept mementoes had suddenly seemed wrong in the new place and she'd thrown them away. She hadn't said what she was doing. Jo had found them in the bin, picked them out and hidden them in one of her own drawers under her jerseys: shells, felt mice, rings from Christmas crackers – nothing bigger than her now full-sized thumbnail. The objects had hardly covered the bottom of a plastic bag, because, although numerous, they were minute. She had kept them for nearly a year. Then she had thought she was being silly and had got rid of them. That was the last of Ella's tidiness. She never arranged her possessions again.

The flat they moved into was part of a low terraced house, further back from the sea, yellow stock brick – similar to the East Greenwich house where Jo had grown up. It had the same orientation – the hall to the right and the front room to the left. Jo hadn't even had to think about which path to walk up, as she would have done had it been the house next door. She had come home, though without the welcome party.

The entrances to the upstairs and downstairs flats were side by side at the end of the narrow hall. The builders had nailed a piece of plasterboard over the old door to the front room. On the inner side, they had left it looking like a door, only without the handle. When Jo viewed the ground-floor flat with the estate agent, she caught herself trying to get out that way, putting her hand out to turn something that wasn't there. She hadn't got far, she thought, ending up in a sliced-up version of her childhood home. She had wondered which half of the house to go for. It had seemed arbitrary. She liked to let a decision settle – to forget about it and then hope the answer would come to the surface, like cream on the old bottles of full-fat milk, but there hadn't been time for that. She and the children had needed somewhere to live. The estate agent had pointed out the good points of both halves and told her that other clients were interested. She had thought about feet crossing the floor above and cooking smells rising from below, as if there had been an extra intermediate floor designed especially for her, with nothing but disadvantages. She had imagined the interested clients. Up and down. She had seen them in her mind's eye: both men. The first was a bit good-looking and a bit ugly, with even teeth and said hullo when they met, in a neutral kind of way, and the second was rather similar. Her opinion of men was at a low point. In the end, she had chosen upstairs. If

Annie had been her only child she would have had the flat with the garden, but Ella and Rob were too loud. Their voices would have travelled the length of the block. There were enough rooms for them to have one each as a bedroom, though Annie often ended up getting into Jo's bed in the night. They made do without a sitting room. The kitchen, off the first half-landing, had space for a table and chairs and an armchair.

The ground-floor flat had been occupied a few weeks later. A couple moved in. Dan and Megan. They didn't cook, or not thoroughly enough to cause rising smells, and they made no noise indoors, just discreetly revved their motorbike when they left for work in the morning. They had a text above the number-plate that said The Kingdom of God is Within You. Luke 17: 21. Their silence made Jo self-conscious about her children. She hadn't realised how disagreeable they always got in the hour before they ate, clumping about the place, falling out with each other. They hadn't improved with age. She had tried to keep them quiet.

'Mum. The train keeps stopping.' That was Rob.

Jo didn't speak. And she kept her eyes closed.

'Why does it keep stopping?' he said.

Annie, who had settled down, stirred.

'Don't wake Annie,' Jo said.

'Is there a *particular* reason, do you think?'

Jo shook her head.

'What will happen when we get to the next station?' he said.

'Nothing will happen.'

Rob was quiet again. Then he said, 'I wish we could just be there.'

The next stop was a station. There were changes in the train's reverberations that came from being shut in alongside buildings and under a canopy. The colour under her eyelids

13

deepened with the change in light. No doors banged. The train started up again.

'Sit down, Rob,' she said. 'Don't touch the window.'

'I'm not opening it. I just want to look out,' he said.

But she heard him go back to his seat.

'Anyway, how do you know what I'm doing?' he said. 'Why have you got your eyes closed if you're not asleep?'

She didn't reply. I don't want to see anything, she thought, and I don't want to be seen. There had been the short period in childhood when she had believed she became invisible if she hid behind her hands or squeezed her eyes tight. It had left a defiant trace. She couldn't recall the moment when she realised that she could be seen – or whether it was one of disappointment or relief. It was no good asking her children things like that. They claimed not to know what she was talking about.

'Hot drinks in this weather.'

'Sorry, Rob?'

'Hot drinks in this weather. She's got a point.'

Jo thought that was what he had said.

Rob's watch beeped. Jo didn't know which hour it was marking. The train moved slowly and absorbed more heat from the sun. Annie's face stuck to Jo's bare leg and the seat stuck to her thin skirt.

The day had begun all right. Though Jo had been reluctant to leave the comfort of bed, the sky, enticingly blue in the gap over the curtains, had encouraged her. Felpo had been beside her, stretched out long length as usual. There was only a sheet covering them – not tucked in – barely dipping between them. She liked his reckless use of space. Nine months in the womb was long enough to be trussed up, he had said when she had commented on how much room he took up. He was using the rest of his life to recover, he had said. She hadn't been complaining. She wouldn't have wanted to lie there without a part of him touching her. After they made love he always slept where he ended up – on one side of the bed or the other. He wasn't territorial. She appreciated that after all those married years of semi-detached owner occupation.

She had got up and left Felpo dozing. He was lazy as a cat until the moment when he had to move and then fully awake. In the kitchen Annie and Rob were already sitting at the table. The air coming through the open window smelled summery. Her bare feet felt at home on the floor. Dan and Megan shut the front door, and minutes later revved up their motorbike and sped down the street. Jo put the supper pans into soak and removed an empty wine bottle from Annie's reach. Breakfast was Annie's most exuberant time of day. She disowned her position as the baby in the family and saw herself as Rob's contemporary, engaging him in conversation as soon as he sat down. She tried to keep pace with what he ate, demanding the same amounts, spooning the stuff in, until it filled her mouth – seeping milk on to her pyjamas when she tried to talk. Rob ate his cereal and kept edging away from her, ending up with his chair tipped against the wall and the bowl on his knees. It was hard for anyone else to talk with Annie chattering on. Jo made toast, singeing it under the grill while she fed the goldfish a pinch of multi-coloured flakes. She watched it come to the surface and gulp. Then she cut off the black bits from the toast and told Annie not to fuss. The mornings had felt leisurely since Felpo moved in. He calmed her.

He came to say goodbye at around nine o'clock. He said he wasn't sure when he'd be back – maybe some time in the afternoon if he was lucky. He'd been helping someone repair a boat for the last week. All through the hot spell he'd worked out of doors. He kissed her, then Annie. She enjoyed both kisses – the first on her mouth, the second a surrogate on her daughter's cheek. She hadn't known that he wouldn't kiss her again. She looked out of the window and watched his van pull away.

Two of Rob's friends came round for him, calling up from the street. Rob borrowed some money from her and went out, crashing down the stairs. Annie fell quiet and the only sounds then were the small ones of the chink of plates being put away and Jo's own footsteps crossing the room. Ella switched the radio on in her bedroom but the noise was faint coming through the wall. Jo hung the damp drying-up cloths over the sill. She was happy without noting her happiness, or notching it up. Ella came into the kitchen and then Jo could hear the words of the song because the doors were wide open – but the peacefulness remained. Ella made herself a cup of coffee and sat down. The silence between them, in the absence of small talk, was domestic, not hostile, unaffected by the music which swam through the rooms and out into the street. Jo recognised herself in Ella, the same unsmoothed edges in looks and temperament. She didn't ask questions about the previous evening. Did you have a good time? Where did you go? Why were you late? She and Felpo were already in bed when she heard Ella bang the front door to the flat and come in. She hadn't checked the time. The questions she might have asked were inconsequential enough but would have veered off into spot-lit interrogation even as she spoke. She wouldn't have meant them to sound like that but intention had nothing to do with it. Jo knew when to back off and she had learned when not even to begin. That left a space with nothing much in it for the present.

Ella drank her coffee, sitting with one foot tucked under her. She stared absently at some mid-point on the table. Jo sensed she was contented to be there with her – Felpo and Rob out of the way. The minutes passed. Ella only looked up when Annie squealed and tried to hide under her chair. She watched as Jo grabbed Annie and lifted her over the sink to wash her hands, the warm water splashing over them both, the soap slipping out of reach. She must have been in a good mood, because when she passed the kitchen again later, she called out to say goodbye.

Jo was the last to leave. She went to the shop for the morning, as usual, taking Annie with her. She was only out of the house for three hours.

When Felpo came home in the afternoon Jo was on the telephone to Trevor Lucas, her employer. He had made an appointment to visit a client, Mrs Ena Tiemann, about a house clearance and had scribbled the address down on the back of a second-hand paperback. The stuff for sale had seemed promising but he couldn't find the book.

Jo heard Felpo's feet on the stairs and the click of the key in the lock. He came in and walked to the far side of the room. She was saying 'Did you put a glass down on it? Look again when you've woken up properly. Perhaps you sold the book.' That was Trevor, she said when she put the phone down. Felpo said, 'Of course.' She took it as an easy acknowledgement. She didn't speak like that to anyone else.

She looked across at him, standing a few feet away from her. She was happy to see him – back maybe for the rest of the day. Annie was playing in Ella's room and had fallen quiet; sometimes after lunch she fell asleep. The older two would stay out in the sun. She went towards him. He said something, but he wasn't facing her and she wasn't paying attention – she was thinking about the afternoon ahead, what they might do in it.

He said he was leaving. She heard him that time. But you've only just come back, she said. He said it would be better if he went quickly and would she get out of his way. She might have smiled. She always smiled when she saw him. I mean it, he said. He wasn't standing still any longer, he was roaming about the room. She said, all right then and moved a couple of paces to one side. She didn't know where to move to. He said, right out. Out of the house. Come back once I've gone. She wondered whether to laugh because it was his voice, yet it wasn't his voice and she didn't know what he meant. She might have started to laugh. He picked up the empty wine bottle from the side and slammed it down on the work top so that it shattered – pieces of green glass everywhere. She took a step towards him, thinking of helping, of getting a dustpan. Don't come near me, he said. He dodged round the table. She was between him and the door. She said – as if it were part of the game – I won't let you go, not like this, and she stretched her arms out, barring the way. He put out his hand. At first she thought he was giving her something. She didn't know what he was doing.

It was characteristic of him to offer her absurd choices and even at the moment when she saw what was hidden between his thumb and his index finger she recognised his way of doing things and wanted it back. They would be sitting in the van deciding where to go for a day out. He'd say they could drive to St Tropez or Sandwich. Jo was free to say the impossible one and it hung buoyantly in the air as if they really had chosen it.

She should have let him go, but she couldn't move. She stood with her back to the doorway, her arms out rigid. He came closer. She said nothing – and he flicked his hand down her cheek. The pain was sharp, but it might have been hot – she didn't know which. Annie screamed and screamed from the hallway and that broke it. He ran past, out of the flat. Jo hung over the sink, retching. Annie carried on screaming. Then Ella was there, holding her head, pulling strands of hair off her face, tying them back. Rob was there, running the tap, dabbing her cheek with cotton wool, letting water trickle down her neck, opening a bottle of antiseptic, stinging her with it. They were sitting her down, pressing her head between her knees. They were propping her up, patting her face with a dry cloth, sticking tiny patches of sticking plaster down it, each one like the peck of a bird.

Everything was bright. The heat of the city, dull as concrete, enveloped the train. The woman in the corner opposite had stood up and was struggling with the window, preparing to lean out and open the door. The train was moving, inching along, jolting over the points.

'We won't get out here, Mum,' Rob said. 'We'll go on to the end of the line. Charing Cross.'

'Whatever for?' she said.

'There isn't time to get everything down from the rack. We can't get off just like that. Without planning it,' he said.

'Well, we can try,' she said. 'Come on.'

'You should have woken up before if you wanted to do that,' he said.

Annie was still sitting on the floor slumped against her mother's shins. Jo lifted her on to her feet. The little girl's legs wobbled and splayed then firmed up. She grabbed hold of Jo's skirt and opened her eyes.

'Look, Annie's awake now. Please try, Rob,' Jo said.

She reached up and pulled down the buggy – almost overbalancing with the child hanging on to her. Rob ignored her. The platform, the intermittent station furniture, the station buildings, the signs saying London Bridge, passed slowly by the windows. Then Rob leapt up on to the seat and seized hold of the pieces of luggage, throwing them one after another to the floor.

'Stop that,' she said.

The train was stationary. The woman had finally succeeded in opening the door. She got out. Rob jumped down and grasped as many bags as he could in each hand.

'Get off the train, Mum. Quick. QUICK.' He was shrieking at her.

The crowd on the platform were wedged together. Behind her Rob was shouting and shoving the luggage against her legs. She tucked Annie under one arm and tried to step off the train. A man lunged towards her, forcing her back into the compartment. Rob's cross breath was on her upper back – his voice in her ear. She struggled forward again, pushing against hot bodies, unyielding shoulders – and reached solid ground. She clung on to Annie. A guard

shouted. Doors slammed. A slow rush of air passed behind
her.

Then they were on their own. A nuclear family. That's
what it felt like. Everyone else dead. The platform was
empty.

'Have you time for a small top-up?' Ena Tiemann said.

'Ample time,' Trevor said.

He always said that. They didn't like to be rushed.

'Help yourself, dear,' Ena Tiemann said. 'And while you're up, just pull the curtain across, will you, the light's in my eyes. There. That's enough. We don't want to shut out all the summer sun.'

Trevor sat down again and put his newly filled glass of vermouth on the small polished table in front of him. The room was now sharply divided between brightness and shadow. The line ran down the middle, with his chair on one side and the old lady's on the other. His glass sparkled.

'You've done well, Mrs Tiemann,' he said, leaning towards her. 'To get it all in boxes.'

The old lady looked surprised. She bent forward a little and the pillow that was behind her head slipped out of place. Trevor got up and propped it back up.

'It must have taken a good few hours,' he said.

She thought for a moment, then she said, 'That wasn't me. That was Mother. She wraps everything up in newspaper.'

Trevor nodded. He was used to old people with mothers alive. He felt at home with the notion that, if you waited long enough, the dead returned as if they had never gone. As an idea, it was less alarming than the one that promised you'd meet them in an after-life.

'Did you see her?' Ena Tiemann asked.

Trevor shook his head.

The old lady was looking beyond him now, though not at the wall behind – at a far-away place.

'So, do you know what's there, Mrs Tiemann?' he said. He separated the words slightly.

Minutes passed. They both waited. And Trevor could see that although she didn't know, she didn't want to think about not knowing. It troubled her.

'Worry not,' he said. 'I'll take them away and see what we've got and come back and give you a price.'

She was quiet again and even shut her eyes for a little while. When she came to she fiddled with the sleeve of her blouse until she found the gap where she kept her handkerchief. She pulled it out and dabbed the corners of her mouth.

'Tomorrow, did you say you'd be here again, Trevor?' she asked after the pause.

'Maybe. If there are a lot of small things in there – jewellery and bits – it might take me longer to sort through. I'll definitely be back by the end of the week.'

'You checked the cupboard, didn't you? Nothing left inside?'

'Empty.'

'I could do with the space.'

Trevor nodded.

'I've lived here all my life. In this house. Four, The Summit. Not many people can say that nowadays,' she said.

'No, it's getting to be rare.'

He got up from the armchair.

'I hope you can lift those boxes. Get someone to give you a hand,' she said.

'I'll manage. The car's parked just outside.'

'One of them's heavy.'

'Is it?'

'Got scales in the bottom. Good scales. Government

22

stamped. Dad bought them for Mother. Carried them home all the way up the hill.'

'Worth buying the best,' Trevor said. 'The best lasts a lifetime.'

'Pans there were. Brass. One for the weights and another for the ingredients. Had to put flour in before you added anything sticky – syrup was always sticky. They jiggled up and down. *She* knew how to use them. I never got the hang of it. Hadn't the patience for baking. Rubbed in, creamed. All that.'

'I'm with you there,' he said.

'Put the cloth on for tea. Polish the cruet. She boiled the clothes pegs once a month. Said it made them keep longer. There weren't many that did that.' She shook her head. 'I couldn't be doing with any of those old-fangled ways. As soon as she'd gone, I wrapped everything in the newspaper and put it away in the cupboard. What did I want with it?'

'That's the idea,' he said.

'It's all good as new. Let someone else enjoy it,' she said.

She looked up at him. 'Who did I say did the wrapping?' she said.

'You said you did it yourself.'

'Before that.'

He shrugged his shoulders.

'Did I tell you it was Mother?' she said.

'Maybe. A few moments ago you might have said that.'

'Must be going stupid. I'll tell you something else, Trevor. I swallowed some buttons. They came with a new blouse in a nice little plastic packet. I didn't know what they were. Thought they were my pills. Swallowed them with a glass of water.'

'Easily done. It's the memory. I'm always forgetting things, losing things. I lost your address but then it turned up.'

He bent down and lifted one of the boxes. 'I'll be back for the others in a tick.'

'You'll take them home with you, will you, Trevor?'

'To the shop. But I need to load the car first. I'll wash up the glasses before I go.'

'If someone takes a fancy to something let them have it. Tell them I said so.'

'I'll do that, Mrs Tiemann. Thank you. You're a good woman.'

Every now and then he went on one of these hunting sprees. They usually involved visiting ageing people, mostly women, whom he'd heard were about to go into one of the local nursing homes. He had friendly arrangements with the female owners of Borrowdale, which he thought of as Borrowed Time, and another, which genuinely seemed to be called Fallowfields. They tipped him off about prospective new clients and he would call on them at their old familiar addresses. He commiserated with them about having to cull their treasured possessions and offered to take the surplus off their hands. This was a good idea in theory, but in practice, the old ladies crammed as much as they were allowed, without infringing fire regulations, in the new small space. Their relatives, cleaners and hairdressers took the better pieces, and he was left with things from the apex of the corner cupboard.

He'd been in many rooms like this one. All curtains and carpets and furniture and breakables. Never a window open. They called him round and talked about their possessions. One or two were always singled out for special attention. Valuable, someone or other had told them. That was the word they always used. Not beautiful or unusual. Something that went for ten, twenty quid at the most in the shop. Yet these old women were decent, not grasping. They needed to know it had all been worth it. Often the items they were selling had belonged to their parents. They felt bad about parting with them. They believed that, having been kept for so long, they too must keep them. For decades these objects had stood in exactly the same spot, fixed like eyes, nose or

24

mouth on a face, and rearranging them meant disfigurement. A few, like Ena Tiemann, hid the relics away for years. It took real courage to ditch them. Lois, his mother, had been different. She had known the selling side. She understood what happened to *things* and had gone out like a lady – leaving nothing but a few sticks of good furniture, enough Jardin de Bagatelle to cover the bottom of the scent bottle and a small overdraft at the bank.

The gentility of the shop had ebbed after Lois's death. Trevor hadn't been able to cope with the detail – the drawers slightly open and the inch of lace-edged linen hanging out. The double room with the staircase rising invitingly up the middle had come to look less and less like an over-stocked drawing room and more like auntie's house after a burglary. He had put a notice on the door asking for a few hours' help a day. A WOMAN'S TOUCH, he had written in capitals across the bottom. No one had responded. Then about a fortnight later a woman had called in. She had looked at the books and tried on a few rings from the table. She had eventually come up to him and asked, in a rather starchy way, what the job entailed. 'Entailed' he had repeated and she had started, embarrassed, and told him that this was one of her gran's words, probably not suitable for general use. She had said she couldn't remember ever having used it before. Trevor had warmed to her then and had waved his arms at the furniture and said it wasn't a pet shop, nothing needed feeding. He said that he'd need her for the mornings only. He had a room upstairs where he lived and sometimes slept, and when he did, he liked a lie-in. She had nodded and glanced nervously up the stairs. He had ignored the glance and asked her name. Jo Price. She had said that she had three children and that she might have to bring the youngest with her. He'd said that was fine – he liked kids. She had agreed to the job. She had stayed and talked to him for a while, accepting his offer of a glass of red. He hadn't shown her the accounts.

Jo told him that she remembered Lois, but not well. When Ella and Rob were younger she used to walk aimlessly round the town with them. She said she liked walking by the sea but Ella and Rob jumped off the breakwaters or threw pebbles at targets. Neither of them feared water and they would chase each other in and out of the sea while Jo shouted at them to come back. She wasn't a strong swimmer. They had looked in windows instead. Front rooms with glass ornaments and wheelbarrows made of shells on the sills. Shops selling multi-coloured chakra charts, crystals and incense sticks. Lois Lucas & Son had been like a peculiar house on display – cosy even in summer. They had always wanted to go in, Jo said.

Trevor was glad that he had taken her on. She smoothed out the days for him; opening on time, dealing with envelopes he didn't like the look of. In return he paid her small sums of money from the tin box. She lit the paraffin stove in the winter and opened the back window in the summer. She made herself a cup of coffee, having sniffed the milk to see if it was off. Lois had assembled a makeshift kitchen in the lean-to at the back and had had it properly wired for the sake of the electric kettle. The electrics in the main part of the shop were dicey, but there had never been the money to put them right, nor the incentive, given the chaos that would have been caused by moving everything to lift the floorboards. The lamps with the two-pin, brown Bakelite plugs at the end worked well enough. They were switched on early when the mornings were dark. Having done the washing up from the day before, Jo settled down with the newspaper in one of the tip-up theatre seats that he had taken advantage of when the Winter Garden at Ramsgate had closed. His mother had had something grander, with a good sweep to the legs, but he had sold it as soon as Probate came through and settled his bill at The Dog. This had mounted up to a sum even more staggering than usual, because he had doubled his intake at the time of her stroke and hadn't subsequently got his average down. He had been fond of his mother. She had been a fighter. Almost to the end she had presided – clamped to her surroundings, short of breath but very much alive – a large woman sliding among teapots, picking up strings of amber beads with delicate stubby fingers, rearranging silver on the yellowish chenille cloth that reminded him of his childhood. He never thought about his father.

Trevor drove home and parked outside the shop. Back at Five, the sign said. Well, it wasn't much past. The three chairs and the old trestle table were still outside. He and Jo and Jo's boyfriendo had sat there the other evening, watching the world go by. He hadn't bothered to take the furniture indoors, nor the tatty books stacked on the window ledge. The weather encouraged indolence. He left Ena's boxes in the boot. There would be time for them later. He'd have to clear a space inside first. He unlocked the shop door and propped it open with a brick in a knitted cover. Then he went back out and settled in one of the chairs. Real heat. He let it spread through him. He could be in a Mediterranean backwater. Some hot arcaded empty square. The cars bearing English number-plates rushed past him – the British chart songs and the smell of British American tobacco gusting from their open windows and sun roofs – but he gave half a thought to the South of France. It was that sort of day. Everyone felt happier. Jo had looked happy this morning. She had left early. 'Something nice?' he had asked her. 'Maybe,' she had said.

Out of the corner of his eye he watched a barefooted couple go into the shop. They reappeared again within minutes and stood in the doorway fondling each other. Then they carried on walking down the road and went into Thresher's. A girl wearing a skimpy top stopped and picked up a book, turned to the back, read the final page, laughed scornfully and put it down again.

27

They weren't numerous, the customers, but on a summer's day people wandered in and out – day-trippers, dawdlers and idlers. This time of year was as good as it got. Most were from England – the south-east corner. London was the limit of where they'd come from so Kent was hardly a challenge to them. They understood the language and the prices. Overheard conversations were all too familiar. The weather was identical. Nothing was a novelty. All this must have been a cause for disappointment. But they liked poking round the shop. He had no idea why they bought what they bought. Carpet sweepers, trivets, hat pins, coal scuttles, jelly moulds. Do you remember – Nan had one of those? He had a box of old holiday snaps. The customers thumbed through them – they bought them. Other people's grandads. It beggared belief. These weren't ancestors in gilt frames. They were someone else's relations wearing shorts and standing in the middle of miniature villages, towering over the church spire and the pub. Yet the customers were adults. They had escaped their childhoods and their parents' childhoods – still they went panting back for more.

There had been several weeks of heat now. Even the nights were balmy. Lying on the bottom sheet with no covers – not even waking in the early hours to retrieve the duvet. A perfect temperature. He planned to sit outside in the street until the sun disappeared behind the houses opposite, then walk across to The Dog.

Someone was tapping on the window behind him. He turned round. He hadn't noticed anyone go into the shop. A man waving a Bunsen burner and a credit card. He didn't take credit cards. It said so quite plainly by the tin box. Bloody time waster. He got up from the chair.

4

Ella climbed over the last gate and leant against it, getting her breath back. She had run in a straight line perpendicular to the railway track, through bumpy fields, over gates, between wire fences. From a distance the land had looked flat and tame – easy walking – but at ground level it was hard work. The furrows in the cultivated parts were deep and the wrong distance apart for ordinary steps. She had had to leap or tread clumsily, up and over. For the last half mile she had struggled uphill, passing through saplings and shoulder-high nettles and patches of mud. Gradually she felt the pulse in her head and chest quieten. She leant down and wiped her face with the bottom of her T-shirt, then she reached in her bag and took out a cigarette and a box of matches. The road facing her was tarmaced but narrow, with a dark hedge on the far side. She lit the cigarette and leant more torpidly against the gate. In fits and starts, she began to register things: the whirr of a small plane high overhead, an ache in her right wrist where she'd steadied herself when she jumped, boys yelling in the distance. And with these came, and also in fits and starts, other symptoms of consciousness: memories of the packing up, the minicab hooting outside in the street and half-formed decisions to walk to a main road, look for a signpost, find her way back.

She went along the lane, surprised at how little effort it was to walk on a made-up road, in spite of her aching legs. Cars passed, but she ignored them and made no attempt to keep close to the side. They had to give her a wide berth. When she came to a junction she turned left, though there were no road signs to show the way. Traffic was moving fast in both directions. She walked almost as carelessly as before and several drivers hooted at her. After about half a mile she came across a concrete shelter. It had no obvious purpose but she stopped there. At the back of the shelter was a bus timetable. One bus an hour it said – nothing on Sundays. She waited.

By the time she was on the bus, Ella was more or less grounded. It was as if the jump from the train had lasted an hour and she had only just landed on her feet. The landscape she saw from the window was familiar, although she'd never seen it before. It was that intermediate territory, which wasn't home, but had the same mix of houses, the same type of lampposts, the same signs advertising a Psychic Festival in Deal, or a Massive Factory Sale of leather jackets in Dover. August Bank Holiday. Hadn't that been and gone?

An elderly woman sitting across the aisle leant across and tapped the handrail.

'Hang on at the next corner, dear; this driver always makes you fly off the seat. I try not to get him, but I had to catch the late bus today because of visiting my sister. Poor girl doesn't know herself any more. Confusion, that's what it is. Don't get old, sweetheart. Here we are, it's coming up now.'

The bus lurched round the corner at high speed, ploughing into the adjacent hedgerow and crunching off branches and twigs. Ella held on, in spite of herself, but she kept facing forward.

'You're not travel sick, are you?' the old woman said. 'You look pale. Not that you'd need to be. This one would turn anyone's stomach.'

She studied Ella's profile.

'I've seen you somewhere, haven't I? Aren't you a waitress at Bettine's?'

'No,' said Ella.

'Must be a shop, then. Do you help in a shop along there?'

'No,' said Ella, more loudly. She had her mother's instinct for denying things spontaneously, rather than revealing herself. It saved a lot of trouble. She got up, walked to the back of the bus and sat down on the furthest seat. The driver glanced in his mirror to check up on her, but the woman didn't turn round. Ella put her feet up on the seat in front, ankles crossed.

She got off the bus at a stop by the recreation ground. It was deserted, as usual, although it was the school holidays: a flat piece of scrubby land with individual stems of ragwort and some other straggly wild flower bristling out of it and a few swings stranded on concrete at the far end. She walked along a path until she came to a group of about twenty houses, each with a garage where a front room might have been. No one was about here either. She went up to one of the houses and rang the bell. She hoped she had got the right house. The bell played a short tune. She pressed her face to the glass and tried again, though she wasn't ready to see anybody. Vince opened the door. She stepped back and swallowed experimentally, as if she'd taken the wrong medicine and hoped there was still a chance it hadn't gone down. Vince peered at her.

'Were we supposed to be doing something? I wasn't planning on going anywhere,' he said.

'No,' said Ella.

Vince leant against the door post and Ella thought for a moment he had forgotten she was there. He was wearing a hat. He knocked it towards the back of his head.

'What have you been doing? I haven't seen you around,' he said. 'But there and again, I haven't been out much.'

Ella looked past Vince's shoulder into the hallway and Vince looked over her head at the houses across the street. They were both silent.

After a few moments, Ella said, 'I wanted to ask a favour.'

'What's that?' he said.

She could hardly remember.

'What's the favour?' he said.

'I need somewhere to stay,' she said. 'Do you think your mum would let me? I mean, it's not desperate. I'll find somewhere else.'

'Tonight?'

She nodded.

'Well, you could've. Like, last week wouldn't have been a problem, but not now.'

'Not now?' she said.

'My brother's back. He got chucked out of his flat again. Something to do with an electricity meter. I haven't got a room to myself any more.'

'I don't need a bed. I'm not fussy,' she said.

'My stepdad's back, too.'

'That wouldn't matter though, would it? I wouldn't get in his way sleeping downstairs.'

'That's the trouble, though. He's sleeping downstairs. That's as far as he got.'

'I suppose I could ask your mum,' she said.

'She's not here,' he said.

'Later,' she said.

'Don't even think about it. She's brewing. She never expected to get them both back, especially not on the same day.'

'It's still warm,' Ella said. 'There's always the beach.'

'Ray wouldn't be up for that.'

'I meant me.'

She turned away from Vince and looked in the vague direction of the sea. It was only about half a mile away, but nobody would have known.

'I wouldn't mind coming indoors,' she said. 'I'm really thirsty.'

'Ray's in there. But come if you want.'

Ella followed him up a steep, narrow staircase. The smell

was intense – like her gran's catarrh pastilles but sharper and fruitier. She had only been to Vince's house once before. She couldn't remember it smelling. She put her hands on either wall, as if to push them away, because it was too soon to close in on family life, even though it wasn't her own. The kitchen door at the top of the stairs was open. Vince went in first.

A man was leaning over the kitchen table with his head covered in a towel. He gasped on his indrawn breath and exhaled loudly. Ella took a step backwards.

'Is he going to throw up?' she said.

'I wouldn't have thought so,' Vince said. 'This is Ella,' he said, raising his voice.

A wide wet face materialised from a wreath of steam.

'Hi, Ella.'

'Hi,' she said.

'I don't know what that stuff is,' Vince said. 'I suppose he's got something the matter with him.'

Ella went to the window and stared out at the town pigeons massed on the opposite roof. Flight had ended uncompromisingly for them too. They looked as if they'd never move again; mutations of the grey composition slates.

'Nan got him shifting the furniture round yesterday,' said Vince. 'I think he's got backache.'

'Bad luck,' Ella said.

'Did you want a cup of tea?' Vince said.

Ella seemed not to hear him.

Ray rubbed his face with a corner of the towel. 'I don't know what he's on about. Dust. I breathed in dust when I moved the flaming wardrobe. What you got that hat on for indoors?' he said, blinking at Vince. 'Boy's a banana.'

He leant back over the bowl and began deep breathing again, long gasps on the in, and slow retches on the out. The towel shuddered.

'We'll go and sit in the other room,' said Vince. 'Let Ray get on with it.'

33

'What about the tea?' Ella said.

'No,' Vince said. 'Forget it.'

They shut the door and went into the living room. The television was on. A woman was demonstrating how to paint gold stars on the inside of a bath. Vince bent down to switch her off.

'Leave it,' Ella said. 'I don't mind.'

She sat cross-legged on the floor and started to pull at the loops in the carpet. Vince turned the volume to nothing. The sun was so bright that the picture was nearly invisible. From time to time bare arms gesticulated, veering across the screen.

'So, what's been going on?' Vince asked.

He leant against the sofa. He stretched out his legs, pulled the hat off and jiggled it from one hand to another.

'Nothing. Everyone's still away on their holidays,' she said. 'Maybe some of them will come back this weekend.'

She didn't have a particular friend she depended on – not a boyfriend or a best girl friend. The group of girls she was with at school formed and re-formed. Sometimes she got bored and drifted away to spend time with Vince who was one of the loners in the year below. She liked Vince but no one else could see the point of him.

A long thread came right out of the carpet. She tried to tuck it back in. She kept her head down and hoped Vince hadn't noticed.

'Why did you want to stay?' he said.

She thought for a moment and then picked on a formula substantially true. 'Mum and her boyfriend had a row. A bad one.'

Vince knew what a row was. He nodded.

'She's packed up and gone. With my brother and little sister,' Ella said.

'Gone where?'

'To my gran and grandad in London. Well, they're my

great grandparents, but we call them that – the same as Mum.

Her mum was killed in a road accident and they brought her up.' She paused. 'I said I wouldn't go.'

'Don't blame you. He's got a funny name hasn't he?'

'Who?'

'The boyfriend.'

'How do you know that?'

'I don't know. I think I met him once. Velcro, or something.'

'Felpo,' said Ella.

'That's it,' said Vince.

'I can't believe you remember him,' she said.

'It was just the name. I'd know your mum again, though. She looks just like you.'

Ella glanced at Vince suspiciously, then stared at the television screen as if suddenly absorbed by it. She was disconcerted by other people's recollections of her. Storing up information was how she thought of it. Though she remembered all sorts of random facts about *their* lives. Minutes went by and Vince leant forward for the remote control to turn the sound back on for her. Ella shook her head and turned towards him again.

'His real name's Phil Phelps; it wasn't wild enough.'

Felpo had told her his real name because she'd asked. Her mum had given her a look, but she hadn't seen anything wrong in asking. If she or Rob had suddenly announced they were going to call themselves Roberto and Eloise, Jo would have told them not to be so stupid – she'd have said they were lucky to have names at all.

'What was the row about?' Vince asked.

'No idea. I wasn't there. Can't you stop fiddling with that hat? It's annoying me,' she said.

'All right,' he said.

He put the hat to one side. 'What did she say had happened?'

'She didn't really speak. She was in a kind of trance.'

35

'Pathetic,' Vince said.

Ella shrugged her shoulders.

'You can stop at home without them, though, can't you? You don't mind being on your own,' he said.

She shook her head.

'Is there something wrong with your wrist? You keep rubbing it,' he said.

'Must have bashed it. It's nothing to worry about. Just hurts a bit.'

She moved her hands apart quickly and placed them on either side of her, palms down. She knew Vince was looking and didn't raise her head.

'Velcro's still hanging around indoors, is he? Boot him out,' he said.

'I don't know where he is.'

'You think he'll come back?'

'I don't know. He didn't take his stuff with him. He took the van though. Mum thinks he won't come back.'

'Get the locks changed. Your mum should have done that. Ray would have sorted it if you'd asked. Replaced the entire door and fixed a new tune for the bell. He did that when my brother borrowed his car without asking. Kept him busy for hours, whistling with screws between his teeth. I had a really nice day. It would have been a bit of excitement for him, locking out your mum's boyfriend.'

'It wasn't like that. We couldn't talk to her. She trailed round indoors, picking things up and dropping them in bags. My brother started to join in. He's that type – knows what he's got to the last end of pencil. He wasn't going to leave any of his precious possessions.'

'Sad,' said Vince. 'What about the neighbours?'

'We haven't really got any. There are just the people downstairs.'

'What's wrong with them?'

'Christian,' she said.

'What about your dad?'

36

'No,' she said. 'I don't want to go and stay with him. Can you lend me a fiver?'

'All right,' he said. 'But I need it back for Saturday.'

'Where is it?'

'In my room somewhere.'

'Go on then.'

Vince got to his feet.

'And could I have some food, once your stepdad's got himself off the washing-up bowl?' she said.

'The fridge is full of crap, now he's back, but I'll try and find something,' he said.

Ella left the house as soon as Vince's mother came home. Lauren didn't smile or say hullo. Her hair was wet from swimming and she was carrying plastic bags full of shopping. Ray had turned up the volume of the sports results so it was hard to hear anyone speak. Vince looked ill after eating oven chips and apple sauce too quickly. He didn't try to persuade Ella to stay on longer. He came down to the front door, though, and saw her out. On his instructions, she found the stile behind the recreation ground and walked along the footpaths that led to the sea.

She sat down on the upper part of the beach where the pebbles were dry. It was an empty time of day. The sea was turning pale and opaque, paler now than the sky. The horizon was a white vacant line. Through narrowed eyes she saw the boats as silhouettes without depth, like dark paper cut-outs. It was possible to forget where she was. She pretended that she was somewhere on the other side of the world, not hemmed in by Calais and the northern coast of France. The little kids had gone back to eat and watch television and the late lot hadn't arrived – the before-bed dog walkers and the teenage lovers with nowhere to go but the shadows of the breakwaters. Ella knew their habits. She spent a lot of evenings on her own wandering along the shore. She took off her shoes, picked them up and walked down to the water's edge, then along, in the shallows, on the shingle. London seemed far away.

The others would be there now. Gran and Grandad would be pleased to have them, but worried by the suddenness, failing to hide either the pleasedness or the worry, letting both come out in the wrong ways. She wasn't with them, but she knew what it would be like. That back room where they ate so real, clear as a dream, the look and the smell of it, the dark green curtains with roses on, steamed limp by years of plain boiled vegetables. She knew what they would be talking about, not just the words, but the words behind the words.

Lovely to have the family all together again, like Christmas, like the days when we made all the decisions and everyone was happy as Larry. We won't ask, but we don't have to, the question lives with us. Do you have any plans, any you-don't-have-to-tell-us-now plans, we-wish-you-were-happy plans that will guarantee that we'll never have to fret about you again?

Ella picked up a pebble and threw it out to sea. It was a good throw. She couldn't even hear or see where it fell.

5

'Have another potato,' Dilys said.

'No, Gran, I couldn't,' Jo said.

'You don't seem to have eaten much, dear. You'll have another, won't you, Rob?'

Rob's hesitation was taken for agreement and his plate was revived with extra potatoes. He made the face of one overwhelmed.

'You don't have to eat them, Rob,' Jo said.

'Leave him alone, Jo, he's growing,' Dilys said. 'You could do with eating more, filling out a bit. You needn't worry about getting fat. You're not the type. It's ageing, losing weight. The skin stops fitting without a bit of flesh.'

'I'm not worried,' Jo said.

'You need to keep an eye on your mother. Get her to look after herself a bit,' Dilys said to her great grandson.

Rob kept his head down and focused on the side of his plate, which was reassuringly empty.

'He does look after me,' Jo said.

'All this eating out of the fridge they go in for now, it doesn't do any good. Families should sit round the table,' Dilys said.

Her position at the table allowed her to look square on at Jo's face. Jo knew what her grandmother was looking at.

'Did you go and see the doctor?'

Jo didn't reply.

'Did she, Rob?'

Rob shrugged his shoulders. 'I don't know. I don't think so. There wasn't time. But we put some stuff on it.'

'You should have had it seen to properly and taken something for it,' Dilys said.

'Taken what?' Jo asked.

'Painkiller. Something to stop infection. Something for shock. You never did like taking things. How deep is it?'

'Not very.'

'Tripping over like that and catching your face on the corner of the stove. I still can't see how you came to do it. What time of day was it?'

Jo said nothing. Underneath the table she gripped her left hand with her right till it hurt.

'How's the seaside?' asked Geoff, putting his knife and fork together and laying his hands on his knees. He had left a potato and there was still some meat on his lamb chop. He never cleared his plate when life was difficult. He and Rob had had the chops, Dilys and Jo the fishcakes, meant for their Saturday supper. The family had, after all, arrived unexpectedly. Dilys never ate fish on a Friday in deference to her chapel-going ancestors. Her mother and father, her grandfather with his watch chain and white whiskers, the minister of the Congregational chapel she had been taken to as a child. She carried on taking notice of them although they were dead.

'You know, it's funny your ending up at the seaside, Jo, and your gran and I retired and still in the smoke. It's us retired ones who're supposed to be by the sea,' Geoff said.

'Yes, you've said that before,' Jo said.

'Seen anything of Peter?' he said.

'Not really. The kids see him,' Jo said. She wished she'd let him dawdle on.

'Never could make any sense of that,' he said.

'Someone should have got a heavy object and knocked some sense into him,' Dilys said.

Jo flinched and looked across at Rob, who was still

cheerlessly tackling his potatoes. The time she most felt a bond with Peter was when her grandparents started on about him.

Dilys seemed to gather her thoughts to say something more conciliatory. A look of unaccustomed sophistication crossed her face.

'We can't all choose right the first time,' she said.

'I'll clear away,' Jo said.

'No, you stay there. You're on holiday. You're to have a good rest. Besides, we're not finished. I've got the pie to bring in.'

Jo sat there. The apparent reasonableness of her grandmother's wisesaw was shocking. The burden of choosing bore down on her, not just the first, but the next and the next. As if potential lovers and husbands appeared in a kind of identity parade and when you messed it up they lined up again. God, not him again. Did anyone get better at it?

'You fetch in the pie, Dilys. I'll clear away,' Geoff said.

Jo heard them moving about, the clatter of plates, the oven door opening and shutting. They came back to the table. Dilys put the dish down and the pie breathed out hot fruity vapours.

'I forgot the cream,' Dilys said.

Jo watched her go back to the kitchen. There was one step down between the two rooms and Dilys stopped on the edge, as if contemplating a precipice. Soon, she'll be afraid of the stairs, Jo thought. Then what will happen?

They were all sitting down again. Dilys looked happier. It had offended her that they had had to eat different things. Choice for pudding was acceptable, though, in this case, there wasn't any, because she hadn't had warning.

'You'll have some pie?' she said.

'Just a small piece. No, smaller than that,' Jo said.

'Rob?'

'No.' It came out too loud. 'Thanks.'

'Well, you can change your mind if you want to. Cream?'

'No, thanks, Gran,' Jo said.

'It doesn't harm you, you know, darling.'

'No, I know that.'

'You have a bit, Rob, in the middle of the dish.'

'No, Gran.'

'Please yourself. I'm not forcing you.'

Geoff lifted the jug of cream in the approximate gesture of a toast.

'It's lovely to have you all here. Under one roof.'

'No Ella, though,' said Dilys. 'It's not the same without Ella.'

There was a pause while they all thought of her. She was almost conjured up. She would have glared at them and disappeared behind her hair. Rob looked across at his mother, but she avoided his eye.

'Where did you say she was?' asked Dilys.

I didn't, Jo thought, and aloud she said, 'She wanted to stay behind with her friends.'

'As long as she's all right,' said Geoff.

'She's got some nice friends, has she?' asked Dilys.

'Just normal kids. You know.'

'She helps out at Lois Lucas's too, you were saying,' Dilys said.

'Every now and then.'

'She seems young to be working,' Dilys said.

'It's only informal, a bit of pocket money. Nothing to get excited about. It gives me a lie-in at the weekend.'

Jo pushed back her chair. She had left most of the pie.

'Rob and I'll do the washing up,' she said.

'No,' said Geoff, 'That's my job. You sit and talk to your grandma. She doesn't often see you. Rob will give me a hand.'

Dilys smiled and patted Jo's arm. 'That will be nice. We'll go and sit in the other room.'

'I'm fine here. Really. Let's not move,' Jo said.

The idea of relocating and stimulating a new, more

vigorous line of questioning appalled her. More of the same seemed simpler and, with any luck, shorter. She knew where her grandmother's edginess came from. Dilys had a nose for ruin. *She* would rather have been dead, than sit on a train looking wretched. The grubby child on the floor, the bag-lady luggage, the fresh scar down the face, the attitude so detached that a girl – one of her great grandchildren – had jumped out between stations. Even recalling the scene seemed dangerous, as if Dilys would get a glimpse of the train compartment through the back of her head.

Jo thought, what has happened to me would never have happened to her. *She* would have known, for a fact, that behaving as I started to behave six months earlier – and behave would be exactly the word she'd have used – would lead to being stared at by a stranger on the train. Dilys didn't acknowledge there was Anyone There, but she abided by the rules set by those who thought there had been. They had all moved on to a less personal billing arrangement. No one called to check the numbers, but they had to pay just the same, she believed that.

Rob and Geoff began to sort out the dishes.

'Don't use the tea cloth for the pans, Rob,' Dilys called out. 'There's an old towel for that.'

She settled herself into her chair as if she meant to stay there. 'So how is the shop, then?' she said.

'Just about ticking over,' Jo said.

'Got some nice things, has he?'

'Not really. The good stock was Lois's and that's mostly gone. Trevor doesn't seem to bother. He doesn't go looking properly.'

'Needs a bomb under him,' said Dilys. 'I expect you do your best. I'd like to meet him one of these days. You've never mentioned a wife.' She looked sharply at her granddaughter. 'Or is he not the marrying kind?'

'Not particularly,' Jo said. 'Though probably not in the way you meant.'

'You get on with him though?'

'Yes,' Jo said.

'Do *you* ever think about it?'

'What?'

'Marrying again.'

'No.'

'I expect you get some interesting types come into the shop.'

'Not many.'

'It only takes one.'

'One what?'

'One interesting one.'

'The interesting ones are women,' Jo said.

She looked with longing into the kitchen. Rob and Geoff were free to restore order, walk to and fro, crash the pans, disappear into the steam. She couldn't sit there any longer.

'They've nearly finished,' she said. 'I'll go up and see if Annie's asleep, before Rob goes to bed.'

'You'd hear her,' said Dilys.

'I'll go and make sure.'

'Let sleeping dogs lie, was always my motto.'

Jo got up.

'She was very quiet, our baby girl,' Dilys said. 'I don't think we heard her voice once.'

'You will,' Jo said.

'She wouldn't let you out of her sight. I thought she'd grown out of that,' Dilys said.

'She was tired. She'll get used to you.'

'I should think so, darling. She'll be different in the morning. Funny little thing,' Dilys said.

Jo went upstairs into the small back bedroom. A triangle of light from the landing extended through the open door. Beyond it, Annie was tucked up in a sheet, one hand loose beside her face, where it must have fallen when her thumb dropped out of her mouth. Jo touched her cheek. Her face was the same as last night and the night before – untroubled. Maybe she had already forgotten what she had seen that afternoon. Jo drew the curtains slowly so as not to make a noise and turned down the cover on Rob's bed.

She went out on to the landing and listened. She heard the burble of voices on television and her grandparents putting things away in the kitchen. She closed the bedroom door carefully.

'I'll make a cup of tea,' said Geoff.

'Don't make one for me,' Jo said.

'I'll go and shake the cloth then,' he said.

Dilys was folding up the day's newspaper and putting it in the bin.

'Look, I'll finish off tidying up, as I'm sleeping down here,' Jo said.

'It's all done,' said Dilys. 'Geoff only needs to lock up.'

'I'll do that,' Jo said.

'No need,' he said.

'I wouldn't mind some fresh air,' she said.

'Fresh air,' said Dilys, turning round and looking at her granddaughter. 'If you want to use the phone, dear, you're welcome to. We've got a perfectly good one here.'

'That's not what I said. I didn't mean go out like that. You can lock up the front. I'll walk round the garden.'

'That won't take long,' Dilys said.

'You won't see what's out,' Geoff said.

'You can show me tomorrow,' Jo said.

'It hasn't been a bad year,' he said. 'All that rain we had in the spring. It was good for the roses.'

Dilys gathered up her bag and her cardigan to take upstairs.

'Rob's watching the TV. Turf him out when you're ready for bed,' she said.

'He's all right for a while,' Geoff said.

'I hope you'll be comfortable. I wish you'd let him sleep

45

down here. Boys his age can get to sleep anywhere,' Dilys said.

'I'll be fine,' Jo said.

'If I'd had a bit more notice I'd have got myself organised,' Dilys said.

'I know,' Jo said.

'We're just glad to see you. Don't forget to put the bolt across, love,' Geoff said.

Jo waited until her grandparents had gone upstairs, then she opened the back door and went out. The air was still warm, and in spite of the murky London sky, the stars were visible. She stood looking at the dark backs of the houses, the even pattern of jutting out and bitten into of the terrace, which meant house to her more than anything plainly symmetrical. A few windows were without curtains. They lit up the deep outdoor passages formed by the back extensions. By day they had always been gloomy places for the frightening parts of made-up games. She could remember feeling brave and cold, venturing down there, and the relief of rushing back into the light. She envied her earlier self the knack of shedding an unwanted state of mind in an instant. The mechanism had clogged up along the way. She remembered how it had been but she couldn't do it.

She was worn out, though not in quite the same way as before. She had had to rouse herself to cope with the talking. She couldn't sit there, dumb, with her head on the table. The questions family asked were of a different weight from other people's – loaded, even the random ones. She needed, mentally, to keep her arms whirling round so that they landed beyond her. Even avoidance took effort.

She glanced up at the back windows. Rob would go to bed soon. He was tired too. She hoped Annie would sleep until morning. She walked back to the house and looked through the window. The kitchen looked strange, as rooms do when seen from the outside. The fittings were old, not as clean as they used to be. Her grandparents couldn't see as well these days, and some of their elbow power had gone. The things on the shelves were familiar, but had lost the significance they had had when she was young. The dish in the shape of a lettuce leaf, which needed scrubbing in the crinkles. The fruit bowl with blue dragons chasing round it, which she used to make wishes on. Now, they weren't so different from the chipped china and glass in the under-a-pound box in Trevor's shop. The most recent object was a picture she had painted at school – cooking apples piled in a dish. Dilys had taken a fancy to it and had it framed. Jo had given up art soon afterwards – when she left school, in fact. She hadn't even thought about picking up a pencil until she began working at Lois Lucas & Son. Then, something about sitting there, without much to do, reminded her. The peace and disorder of the school art room came back to her. There was no shortage of still life in the shop and the dust was a challenge; it blurred the edges. The new drawings were tentative to begin with, of wispy thinness; less bold than the cooking apples. Then they grew darker. It was as if she were gouging out lines and shapes on a block. She took a chance, identified the light, but didn't know how the shadows would fall. It was only when she finished that the blackness remaining made sense.

She went back indoors, shivering slightly. She felt for the key and turned it, then shot the bolt into place.

6

Ella put her shoes back on and carried on walking – along the shore, past the golf links and the bungalows, until she was within sight of the beacon at the mouth of the River Stour and the gasometer on the far bank. She walked for the moment without feeling troubled, or, at least, her troubles flowed in and out without getting clumped into knots. It wasn't too bad, the cut on her mother's face, more like a deep scratch, really, though it stayed in Ella's mind like a sliver of moon in the sky. She came this way most evenings when she wasn't out with friends. She didn't like being at home. Even when she stayed in her room she heard Jo and Felpo through the door talking and laughing in the kitchen – and the gaps when they went silent. She hated the gaps. Her mum always used to eat with them but then Felpo started to cook and the two of them always ate late. He said the cooking was for all of them but she didn't like the smell or the way he tipped everything in the pan together. She lit candles in her room and sprinkled scented oil on them but the cooking smells came under the door. If she was out of the flat she didn't know what they were doing. When they ate or when they went to bed, when they used the bathroom. Time passed and she didn't have to think about them.

She turned round and headed back south along the beach. She stayed calm, not minding that the sun had set and that the air was finally cooling. Things looked different in darkness. The colours changed. The glow from a tropical fish tank in one of the windows was bluer and brighter. The sea was like dirty copper.

Her courage left her when she was back on the stretch of beach closest to home. She was tired and her arms were beginning to feel cold without a jumper. She rubbed them to get rid of the gooseflesh. The pebbles had used up the heat from the day: cold water seeped from them. The damp came through her shoes. She spent about ten minutes beside the water's edge trying to guess the sea's movements. She thought that she would choose a pitch and settle down for the night once she had worked out where the high tidemark was likely to be. Though, since she had no blanket or newspaper – nothing to put between her and the pebbles – settling down just meant lying on the ground.

In the distance, beyond the stack of deck chairs, Ella saw an old man dragging a low box on a piece of cord. He pulled it behind him as if it were a kind of sledge and, every now and then, when it got stuck, he turned to face it and heaved with both arms from the front. There was no one else, just the old man. The shoreline stretched away behind him, interrupted by the breakwaters. She turned her back on the sea and walked back up the shelves of the beach, placing her feet carefully, so that the old man wouldn't hear her – but the crunching she made got louder and faster as she moved further away from the sound of the waves. The shingle ended suddenly with a wall. Ella pulled herself over on to the pavement. She waited for a burst of traffic to pass, then crossed over and turned into the first of the smaller streets behind the promenade. She stopped and lit a cigarette, then walked down the middle of the road between the parked cars.

She forgot the old man with the box and felt merely depressed. She had thought of herself as the kind of person who could sleep rough, though she had never tried until then. Even saying the word, rough, to herself, marked her

49

out. Bus shelters, shop doorways – just pairs of words. Since she hadn't been brave enough, she felt let down. She took the usual route home. Beyond the town cottages was a short row of shops, the end one of which was the junk shop, Lois Lucas & Son. Ella took a step back and looked up. The curtains of Trevor's upstairs room were closed. She reached into the bottom of her bag for her keys. As she put the key in the lock she pressed her face to the glass in the door. The street lamp across the road gave a queasy light, revealing the forms of the items of furniture and the stacked-up boxes, the glints of the glass and the brass. She went in.

The shop felt different at this time of night. Enclosed and silent – somehow more inland. By day, there was a sense of the sea not far away; seagulls and a seaweedy kick to the draught through the open door, but this had vanished. The smell was familiar, but concentrated – musty, like stale tea spiked with alcohol. Breathing it in steadied her. She crossed the floor, careful not to bump into anything, aware of moving between patches of shadow and half-light, and nervous that someone passing might see her. There was the blind at the window which was made of shiny black-out stuff – it squeaked if you tried to move it. She wouldn't make the effort. It was better to be able to see. She went across to the table where Trevor dumped the books when he brought them in from the window ledge at the end of the day. He never had anything she wanted to read. She pulled one of the books out and took it to the front where she could see by the street lamp. She turned the pages of dense type until she reached a passage of conversation. No one could ever have talked like that, not even Herbert and Ivy, or whatever they were called. She glanced at the date at the front. They'd be dead by now anyway, so they were doubly dead, never having lived.

She knew her way round. Somewhere among the clutter would be a cushion or two, maybe a rug. Under Lois's management, Ella would have found enough props for a stage-set bedtime – chaise longue, white lace-trimmed night-dress, silver candle holder – but that was all over. She found an alarm clock in the under-a-pound box and set it for six o'clock; hours earlier than Trevor would saunter down the stairs. She moved a typewriter out of the way, spread out a blanket made of knitted squares on a section of floor furthest from the window and placed a cushion at one end. Having taken off her shoes, she lay down, stretched out on her back and looked up. Directly above her was a stain the size of a man's hand, beginning to flake now and still unpainted – even in the poor light, it was visible. It had appeared at the beginning of March. Her mother would remember the date.

At that time, she and Jo had been getting on not too badly. They annoyed each other but they were still connected. Jo expected her to do things that her friends didn't have to do, such as look after Annie or help in the shop. She didn't mind doing them but, since they were favours, she resented being called unreliable when they didn't quite work out as planned. On that particular Saturday, for example, she had promised to go and open up the shop. The weather was foul. Her room was on the side of the house that was squashed against taller buildings, so, although the curtains dipped at the top because the rail was bent, the daylight hardly changed the look of things if it was a dull day. But apparently it was morning. Someone was banging and banging on her door. Rob was shouting, saying she ought to get up. Who says so, she shouted back. Mum, he said. Why can't she tell me herself, she said. She's got a headache, he said. So have I, she said. Lazy cow, he said. She's a lazy cow, she said. It was the usual sort of argument. Jo would have got the gist of it too. Ella willed herself to get out of bed, switch the radio on, wash her face in the bathroom. Eventually she put on some clothes and went into the kitchen. Annie was at the table eating biscuits. Ella felt sorry for her, sitting there on her own. She scooped her up and took her with her to Lois Lucas & Son.

She and Annie had hardly been there half an hour when Jo showed up. She was out of breath from running and her jacket was pulled over her head against the downpour.

'I thought you were supposed to have a headache,' Ella said.

'I have,' Jo said.

'Why did you come out then?'

'Because I had no idea where any of you were,' Jo said.

'You knew I was here.'

'I hoped you would be but I didn't *know*. You could have left a note. And how stupid was it to bring Annie with you? You've never done that before,' Jo said.

'You weren't awake,' Ella said. 'And Rob had gone out.'

Jo didn't reply. All they could hear was the rain striking the lean-to – loud as beads on a tin plate.

'And look at Annie,' Jo said.

Annie's hair was clinging to her head in damp stripes, making her ears stick out, but she was laughing. She looked fine. A bit of water never did anyone any harm. Jo took her into the kitchen to rub her down.

While she was gone a man appeared at the window jumping from one foot to the other in a kind of dance and miming to be let in. Rain was cascading from the gutter and splashing on to the ground below. Ella ignored him.

'Why doesn't he just come in?' Jo said when she came back.

Ella shrugged her shoulders. 'Some nutter,' she said.

Jo went over to the door. 'It's locked,' she said. 'Did you lock it?'

'Could have done.'

'Why?'

'You said you didn't trust me. Obviously I can't be left on my own here.'

Actually, she hadn't done. Her mum had banged the door so hard behind her it had locked itself. It did that sometimes.

Jo took a deep breath and turned the open/closed sign round before unlocking again. The man came in, smiled at them, said he wouldn't get in the way, and started to wander round the shop. He was skinny and medium tall, wearing jeans and an old black coat with a funny-looking woven bag slung over his shoulder. His eyes drooped slightly at the corners which made him look nervous and pleased with himself at the same time. Jo went through the usual routine – unlocking the cash box, doing Trevor's washing up from the day before, sniffing the milk to see if it was off – though everything she did was louder than usual. Ella knew she wanted to carry on quarrelling but she behaved herself because a stranger was there, watching.

'Nice jug,' the man said.

He was at the back of the room, over by the stairs. He was holding out the jug, trying to line it up to catch drips that were coming through the ceiling. It was quite ugly – bright yellow with a kingfisher as a handle. They hadn't noticed the drips. Jo said that if he wanted to buy the jug he would have to look round and find something else to put under the leak. After a few minutes he said that it wasn't rain coming in. Jo said she knew it wasn't – there was a bathroom up there, not the roof. The whole place was falling apart. He said, sorry, he only knew because the places he lived in always seemed to end up under water. He'd learned to recognise the different types. Leaking water had got a particular smell, hadn't it? A stale, plumbing smell. You walked in and knew straight away. He didn't like the sound either; he had to talk himself into it. Sometimes he took a lot of persuading when water was gushing out like Niagara Falls or he was paddling round like a granny at the seaside.

He was one of those people who never shut up. But Annie was fascinated and kept staring at him. He noticed her staring.

53

'Tigers don't understand water, do they,' he said to her. 'They don't appreciate its good points. I suppose that's why your tiger's stopped in today.'

'I don't have a tiger,' Annie said.

'This is what they particularly enjoy,' he said.

He positioned the jug on the floor, knelt down beside her and moved his thumb in a slow circle. 'You may not think they like their ears flattened, but if you do it right they do.'

Ella stared too then, although she didn't want to. It suddenly seemed that there might really have been a large cat that had come in out of the rain. He smiled when he saw them gazing at nothing.

'Let's find her somewhere more comfortable,' he said.

He looked round the shop.

'That'll do,' he said, pointing at one of the tip-up chairs.

'It's from the Ramsgate Winter Garden,' Jo said. 'It closed down.'

A customer came in. A woman. She was wearing full-on waterproofs, like a fisherman. She stood and watched the man pick up the invisible tiger, stagger across the shop with it and place it on the chair. Then she cleared her throat and said she would like to leave some leaflets about a spring flower event. She called it an arrangeathon. She jabbed one of her pieces of paper at the man and said that he looked like someone who could stick a notice in a window. He said he'd do better than that; he would distribute them personally around the streets. He took the whole clutch from her hand. She said, '*Not* under windscreen wipers, please.' He said he wouldn't dream of it. He said people with his sort of problems always liked a bit of community work.

'Are you still annoyed?' he said to Jo.

'No,' she said.

'Good,' he said.

Then he left.

'What an unusual man,' the spring flower woman said

after he had shut the door behind him. 'Perhaps we could get him involved in the Fun Run.'

The next week he moved in. During the time in between her mum behaved quite normally. She didn't look as if she was planning to fall in love.

after he had shut the door behind him. 'Perhaps we could get him involved in the Fun Run.'

The next week he moved in. 'During the time in between her mum behaved quite normally. She didn't look as if she was planning to fall in love.

7

Jo lay on the sofa and felt the tilt of it and the crenellations in the upholstery that came up through the sheet. As soon as one cluster of noises ended another started up – cars and beeping, clacketty heels and shouts of laughter. There were extra layers of sound in London. You could never guess from the *A to Z* how many people were crammed in the gaps between the streets. She was glad to hear voices. The series of overlapping goodbyes. The household had been peaceful for hours. Her grandparents hadn't talked for long in the room above her. Alone together at the end of the day, they read library books and imposed wordlessness on each other that Jo admired. But she couldn't sleep. The shadows of the furniture, the china plates and the pictures on the walls wouldn't let her rest. They weren't neutral – having been there from the beginning. She had left but they had stayed.

She was hardly ever out this late, though she and Felpo had absconded a few times. They had done it to be somewhere different, away from home. Not the Sandrock Hotel car park, which was a local venue for seducers, but places less flagrant, starrier. Though this was a distinction which Dilys's wardens of conscience – the parents and grandfather, the minister of the Congregational chapel – would have seen as spurious. Jo remembered each occasion quite separately, though they had done the same things. Three times they'd got back in the flat and into her bedroom uninterrupted. On the fourth, the lights had been on indoors. She was afraid that Annie had been crying for her. She had smoothed down her skirt and tucked Felpo's shirt in. It was Ella who was awake though, not Annie. She had locked the bathroom door and refused to come out. Jo tried to talk to her through the keyhole, asking her, pointlessly, if she was all right. She had emerged in the end, saying they could use the toilet if they were quick, so they'd gone in, she and Felpo, one after another, like children allowed to go in lesson time, but only with the teacher standing outside. Then Ella barged back and knelt on the floor. Jo had hovered over her, asking her if she felt sick until Ella said, of course she felt sick, and told her to go away. Jo had gone to bed, leaving her there. She hadn't managed to get to sleep though, even after the cistern stopped heaving and Ella's bedroom door had clicked shut. Felpo knew Jo was awake and had stayed awake too. He had put his arms round her. There had been no need to say anything.

She turned on her side – the side which wasn't sore – trying to find a position she might rest in. It felt strange to be sober. She was used to sharing a bottle of wine with Felpo every evening. They had got into the habit of it. She saw the ludicrous pile of luggage in the middle of the floor and closed her eyes. She could still feel the tightness in her skin, though the sensation was lessening and the sharp pain had gone. She resisted touching the wound – not because she'd been told only to touch her face with her elbow but because she didn't want it to be true. She finally slept. Her dreams were old stock. He was present in the last of them. The same as he always was. Bare feet, old jeans, strong hands, old T-shirt, the dark clumps of hair which would never lie down on his head. He touched her – fleetingly – then the dream moved on. They had nowhere to go and were looking for a place to be alone. Searching room after room in a strange house where all the rooms interconnected. A sick feeling came over her as she surfaced from the dream. Then she slipped out of consciousness again, as into an un-named lake.

Saturday

1

Without a bed to disentangle herself from, Ella came clean out of sleep before the alarm went off, cold and conscious of the floorboards. She checked the time. Five thirty. The moments that usually piled themselves up like bedclothes fell away. She switched off the clock. Her shoes, bag and keys were arranged beside her at eye level. She got up, put the shoes on and kicked the cushion to one side. Then, having picked up the bag and the keys, she opened the door of the shop, locked it behind her and was immediately out in the still air and grey light. The parked cars had a film of dew on them and the sky was hazy, though it wouldn't stay pale. Within an hour it would be blue and the sun would blaze down. She walked down the street to the sea front, moving quickly because she felt cold on the inner side of her skin from waking too early. When she got to the promenade everything was shut. The stalls and the shops were dead. The kiosks, which sold ice cream and cold drinks, looked like crates that were about to be hoisted up on to a container boat and taken across the Channel. The flowers in the middle of the mini roundabout were closed up, showing the dull side of their petals.

Then the pace changed. She had too much time. She waited for the first café to open so that she could get a cup of tea and a packet of crisps, waited for the woman to arrive by car and unlock the municipal toilets, waited for the bus to take her to Dover. She sensed, for the first time, that the beginning of the day was precarious. The woman with the key might roll over and fall asleep again.

She got off the bus and walked up the steep road that climbed out of Dover towards the castle. The houses rose in irregular steps to accommodate the hill, and the cars were forced into low gear. Peter and Tara lived near the top.

Amber, the previous owner of the house, had been a bed and breakfast landlady with exuberant taste. She had dressed up the porch with climbing greenery and tucked coloured lanterns and wind chimes into the leaves. Peter and Tara had borrowed a ladder and taken the decorations down, but the vegetable life remained lush and spiralled round the spaces where they had once fitted, a reminder of more festive times. Amber's personality had gradually been wiped out. The silver paint on the front door, the stripes on the barley-sugar banisters, the bubbling jet in the back garden – they had all had to go. Ella had told her mother about Amber, and Jo had drawn a picture of her – all wild hair and shiny boots. Jo had said that Peter and Tara had used up their only portion of waywardness in leaving their wife and husband, herself and the unknown Steve. Who was Steve? Since then, Jo said, they had gone back to being humdrum.

Ella stood outside the front door, now covered up with a safer paint. Today was Saturday, so her father would be at home. Shopping list, shopping, gym. He would only be at the first stage. His arrangements ran like a child's news written in a school exercise book. I woke up . . . then I . . . then I . . . He crossed off the day's activities as he went along. She didn't know whether, when no one was there to check up on him, the routine blew apart, but she hadn't caught him out yet. She wondered whether he had always been as predictable. She couldn't remember. She hadn't thought of him as abnormal when they had all been together. Once he'd gone, she had looked at him in a different way.

She had carried on seeing him once every two or three

weeks, but her memories of him, muddled up, in the usual way, with family stories and photographs, stopped joining up with the present. Before, the slightly greyer, heavier dad-figure in the old black jersey had been easily swapped with the younger version, who had admired her balancing on the wall by the newsagents and lost her on Deal pier, but the conjuring trick had ended when he left.

She hesitated in the porch, and then knocked. The door opened straight away. Peter and Tara were both standing on the other side of it, dressed for the weekend in similar leisure wear. Tara was holding a clutch of car keys.

'Sorry,' Ella said. 'You're on your way out.'

'Well, we were,' Tara said. 'But not now.'

She smiled and gave Ella a kiss. The front door opened directly into the sitting room, so they were already there, with the sofa and chairs in an instant interior. Peter shut the door behind them.

'How are you doing?' said Peter.

'I'm all right,' said Ella.

The carpet on the floor was spotless and pale. She could never believe how spotless and pale.

'Everything going fine?' said Peter. 'What do you fancy doing?'

'I don't mind,' Ella said. 'I'll fit in with you. I might not stay long.'

Vince's fiver had already disintegrated into small change. She was hoping that Peter had some spare cash.

He switched on the Ceefax news pages. Airport holiday chaos. A child missing in Cumbria. The soundtrack, which had no connection with the written pages, was of splashes and excited screaming. He clicked on to the weather.

Ella looked past Tara's shoulder into the kitchen. It was like the inside of a bathtub, scrubbed, nothing visible.

'I didn't have breakfast. Is there anything to eat?' Ella said.

'Yes, of course,' he said. 'Well, no, actually. There isn't.

We were just on our way to do the weekly shop.' He patted his pocket to see if his wallet was still there.

'There's half a melon,' said Tara. 'One of those small pink ones.'

Peter switched off the television.

'It's going to be another hot one,' he said.

'A piece of toast?' asked Ella.

'No, I don't think even that,' Peter said. 'Ridiculous, isn't it? We don't really buy bread. I can make you a cup of coffee without milk, if you fancy that. I tell you what. I think there might be an oatcake.'

'No, thank you,' she said.

'Sorry,' said Peter. 'It's stupid not having anything in. I mean, people do come round off the stick end.'

'When?' asked Ella.

'Well, since you mention it, it's true, they don't,' said Peter. 'But basically it's a nice idea.'

'We're always seeing people,' Tara said. 'Ella will think we haven't got any friends.'

'We have got friends, haven't we?' Peter said.

'Don't worry, Dad,' Ella said. 'It's not a big deal. Look, I'll come with you, shall I? I can stick some stuff in the trolley.'

Peter looked gratefully at her. 'You sure?'

She nodded.

'Have you got the towels for the gym, darling?' Tara said.

'What for?' asked Peter.

'I thought it was easier if we had the things in the car.'

'We don't have to decide now,' he said.

'You mean we might not go to the gym?'

'I don't know,' Peter said. 'We'll leave it open. Ella's here. We might go out for a bite to eat or something.'

'It's all right, Dad,' Ella said. 'I've got things to do. Let's just get in the car.'

Ella sat in the middle of the back seat to get a view. She

didn't want to stare at either of their heads. Peter started the car and they drove up the hill.

'Have you got the day off?' Tara said.

'Sorry, Tara?' Ella said.

'I thought you worked on Saturday morning,' Tara said, 'at that shop.'

Tara didn't turn round to talk. As soon as they had begun to move she had pulled down the mirror flap above the windscreen and was now squashing her nose to one side with a finger, to look at an invisible blemish.

'Not always,' Ella said.

'How is everyone?' Peter said.

'Usual.'

The road was curvy and Ella remembered how she used to feel when she was little and car-sick. It was just the edge of a feeling.

'Are they doing anything special today?' Peter said.

'Shouldn't have thought so,' Ella said. 'Special doesn't often come into it.'

'Did you remember the list, pet?' Tara said.

'No, it doesn't matter does it?' asked Peter. 'Ella wants things. We'll go up and down the rows.'

Tara snapped the mirror back shut and looked out. They were slowing down. Ella opened the windows on both sides to let in some air, then moved over behind Tara and let her hands trail out in the stream of air. Her fingernails were dirty arcs on the ends of her fingers.

'We don't often get stuck here do we?' said Tara. 'Do you think it's road-works?'

'Could be,' Peter said.

They moved forward slowly. A wasp flew in and out again. Ella sat still. Tara and Peter didn't notice it.

'What's Rob doing? We haven't seen him for a while,' Tara said.

'Not sure,' Ella said.

'He gets on well with your mum's boyfriend, doesn't he? He was telling me,' Tara said.

Ella said nothing.

'They play beach football together,' Tara said.

'Do they?' Ella said.

'Is it true about the kinky van?'

'Don't know,' Ella said.

'Your mum's boyfriend's van. Rob was saying he's painted all angels and flowers over it. Sounds weird.'

'I didn't hear him say that,' Peter said.

'It's different now,' Ella said. 'He's always changing it.'

'So what's it like at the moment?' Tara said.

'Just freaky colours. That time it said "Straight to Heaven with Felpo your Fully Independent Funeral Director".'

'That's a bit sick, isn't it? If you'd just lost someone,' said Tara. 'Felpo, that's right. I wonder where he got that name from.'

They overtook a broken-down lorry. It took a couple of minutes to negotiate. Then the road straightened and they started to speed up. Ella's hair blew across her face. She let it float about.

'Would you say he was creative, Ella? That might be the appeal for your mum. She's quite alternative, isn't she?' Tara said.

'When I was young no one ever said creative,' Peter said. 'They talked about imagination. Teachers used to say you had one if you could think of pictures to draw and stories to write when they couldn't be bothered to think up a title. I was never any good at that kind of thing.'

'I couldn't have stood it,' Tara said. 'You're the next generation, you and Rob, you don't want someone else breezing in and being original all over the place.'

'Ella's always had an imagination,' Peter said. 'I don't know who she gets it from. Not from me, that's for sure.'

They drove in silence for about ten minutes, then joined a

line of cars that were waiting to turn right for the trading estate.

'That bloke in the red Beemer, do we know him? He just smiled at me,' Tara said.

'Shouldn't think so,' said Peter, looking straight ahead. 'But he's got good taste.'

'You sometimes see those photos, don't you?' Tara said. 'Would you trust this man? And you always know. I do, anyway, it's instinctive.'

'How do you check up?' Peter said.

They were edging round the store car park now.

'Oh, I can't remember. They tell you. You turn the page upside down.'

'How do they know? The people who devise the test? It doesn't sound very scientific,' Peter said.

'Your dad's so literal-minded, Ella,' Tara said.

She paused and uncrossed her legs.

'Try to find a space on top, Peter, I can't stand that ramp,' she said.

'I'll do what I can.'

'You just missed one.'

'It wasn't big enough.'

'Well, go round again.'

'Look,' said Peter, 'there isn't anywhere up here. Do you want to get out, Tara, and we'll meet you at the front, by the veg?'

Peter stopped the car just before the entrance to the underground car park. The driver behind hooted. Tara got out, walked to the trolley stack then turned round and waved. Ella looked away. She leant forward and wrapped her arms across the empty front passenger seat. Peter drove slowly down the ramp with his lights on. The bends were tight and each one was streaked with coloured car paint where people had missed.

'*Is* it all right at home?' asked Peter, into the darkness.

'Sort of,' she said.

The mental pictures she saw as she spoke were just that, pictures, framed and at a distance. There were two of them. Rob, Gran, Grandad and her mother, sitting round the table, the jug of water, the vegetable dishes with the green and gold rims, the curtains drawn, the lights on. The other was of their kitchen at home. Jo was lifting Annie up to the sink to wash her hands, saying silly things to her, making her laugh. Her mother's hair was tied back from her face. No one else was there.

'I could do with getting out more,' she said. 'Doing stuff with friends. But it always works out so expensive.'

'What time of day are we talking about?'

'Not late.'

'Are you sure?'

''Course.'

'I sometimes think that your mother hasn't got her eye on the ball. I suppose it's no good asking you whether she has or hasn't.'

'Not really.'

'I never know why there are puddles down here,' said Peter. 'It hasn't rained for weeks.'

He parked the car next to a concrete pillar, shuffled in his wallet and passed some notes to Ella.

'Cheers, Dad,' she said and kissed his left cheek.

2

The light was bright, not early-morning light. Jo heard drilling in the road, shouts above the drilling and the outside voices of people properly awake. Where was Annie? The smell was familiar; furniture polish from a yellow tin, yesterday's cooking fat, trapped dust. She shifted out of sleep and her feet met the end of the sofa. So, she was at home; her first home, the place where the solution hadn't been found but where they still, the three of them, had managed to live.

The day was too far on. Jo was wide awake and anxious. She got up and went over to the window that looked out over the narrow back garden. She undid the catch and unscrewed the bolts. The sliding parts didn't want to move, so she hit both sides hard with her fists. The painted wood budged and she opened the window wide, top and bottom, and let in the London air. It was no different from what was inside – tepid and motionless. She knelt down and rested her arms on the sill.

She had never told Dilys and Geoff anything about Felpo. Not even of his existence. She hadn't wanted to share him. The questions would have started straight away. So where does he come from? That's not his real name then? So he *is* English? Dilys and Geoff wouldn't change. Past attitudes took up most of their mental space. There were a few more recent additions, such as a tolerance of the Tory party that would have shocked their ancestors, but they didn't encroach. The weight for them was all at the beginning.

Their early lives crammed with people, blood relatives, family friends, church ministers – all with firm opinions, generally the same ones. They weren't what they had been – having been filtered through Dilys's mind they had lost their fire. Sin and damnation downgraded to cause and effect.

Where did you meet him, Dilys would have asked, and Jo would have had to reply, at Lois Lucas & Son. Though the pub or the sea front would have been a better choice because, at the mention of Lois Lucas, Dilys would immediately have thought of a man in a navy blue blazer or a tweed jacket who was looking for a Welsh dresser. Not Felpo's style. Whatever Jo said about the shop – joking or despairing – Dilys thought antiques more than junk and the impression never shifted. It was probably her own fault for trying to make the job seem acceptable in the first place. Near home, part-time, a friendly boss whose mother had recently died. She might even have used the phrase bric-à-brac, but she hoped not. Dilys saw what she wanted to see. She and Geoff would never have understood Felpo: his lack of family ties.

He told her that he'd lost touch with his relatives on the Sunday after he moved in with her. They were walking up on the cliffs with Annie – carrying Annie. They had gone in the van to Eastbourne to walk up Beachy Head. They had reached the part of the path where the In Memoriam benches ran out. Engraved with old-fashioned names, they stood looking out to sea at respectable distances apart – dedicated but shunned. No one sat on them. It was the limit of the town excursion. Most people turned back at that point. Jo remembered exactly where they had been because, in her mind, she had connected the benches with the mother he hadn't seen for twelve years, the father last heard of in Plymouth, the brother last heard of in Scotland, the second brother in Canada, half-brothers and -sisters he didn't know where. He talked about them, the ones who were still alive, as if the world were small enough for the chances of coming across them in a bar to be quite high. She felt lucky that he'd touched down in Kent for long enough to have met her. There hadn't been quarrels, he said. He always phoned his mum at Christmas and sent a card on Mothers' Day. He just didn't get on with the man she had living with her. He spoke about past girlfriends in a matter-of-fact way too, indicating that he and they had gone, or grown, in different directions. He had moved around a good deal. She guessed that there had been more of them than he had let on about and that maybe the ends of the relationships hadn't been as pain-free as he had made out. She didn't press him. Some people didn't like raking up the past.

The conversation had to stop when they reached the gorges that the streams made before cascading into the sea. Steps were cut into the steepest slopes but mostly the footpaths slithered down between gorse bushes and brambles. They needed to concentrate on walking, taking it in turns to jump Annie down the steps. The ground was too slippery to carry her. Out in the open again, Felpo didn't seem to have anything else to tell her and she was sorry that they'd been interrupted. She told him about her childhood, instead. She wanted to tell him. With Peter she had played down anything connected with her family or upbringing that wasn't, as far as she knew, within the limits of what normal people would consider normal. She had given the impression that it had all been pretty standard. But with Felpo her memories felt safe. The great upheaval of her life – her parents' death – had somehow been accommodated, bedded into life's structure, its jagged aspects ground down for everyone's sake. She discovered she could dig around a bit without incurring disaster. He didn't have an immaculate family of his own to measure her by.

She told him that she had known about the motorbike accident on the new roundabout from as early as she could remember. Dilys and Geoff had been in their late forties when it happened. She might even have been their daughter by something resembling an Old Testament miracle – but she wasn't. She was Gail's. They had been quite open about their daughter's death. The rest of the information had come later – that Gail, aged eighteen when Jo was born, had never married or left home and that her boyfriend, Jo's father, had been driving the motorbike Gail was on the back of when they were both killed.

Gail was never criticised, she said. She had been much loved – and she had died. No doubt there had been trouble at the time of the pregnancy but this was never referred to. She, on the other hand, had been praised and blamed in the old-fashioned way. Gail had been different from her. She had entertained all the relations – not minding singing in public, or sitting on anyone's lap. There was a photograph of her dressed up as a princess and waving at the camera. Another with the cousins on a birthday picnic – piles of sandwiches and a cake, everyone sucking through drinking straws, their eyes bulging. There was a trouser leg spoiling the edge of the picture, cutting off half of a cousin, but otherwise there were no grown-ups in sight. Jo used to hold up the album and look in the mirror to discern a likeness – that was Dilys's word – but her cheeks were a different shape and that changed everything. No one else in the family had that shape – hollow, then going up and round the corner – only Ella. So the bones of their faces must have come from her father. She might have disliked Gail for being popular if she'd been her sister, but, because she was dead and her mother, she had felt sorry for her and, in a way, relieved, that she wouldn't ever have to disappoint her. She had been envious of her life, though. Picnics for Jo had meant being propped up between Geoff and Dilys in London parks picking off skin from the boiled eggs and drinking still lemon made up in a Thermos flask. No other children. She had got tacked on to the previous generation and there simply weren't any.

Walking with her back to the wind, looking at the chalk land tilting away from them, Jo felt she had regained a

70

carelessness that she had known about as a child but mostly missed out on. She suddenly saw through a clear expanse that had been cloudy up until then. There was something about Felpo that made her not mind seeing with clarity – and it was the not minding that was new. Dilys, Geoff, the mother she knew only from the photograph album, the father who was just a name – though not one that appeared on her birth certificate – she felt she could tell him about them. He listened and laughed at her jokes. He had an open-air kind of laugh. He seemed to grasp the idea of Dilys. He was kind about her. She'd have sorted him and his brothers out, he said. They had needed a firm hand. The only orderly things about the place he was brought up, he said, were the goldfish and the pine disinfectant. Jo imagined a sort of tenement – iron fire escapes and lavatory tiles on the walls of the stair wells, more Dilys's idea of a slum, really – until he mentioned the small house in Stevenage that needed re-wiring and re-roofing. She told him about the tenement. He laughed and said that he often dreamt up the wrong pictures – at least she had the excuse of the missing generation. Having been brought up by her gran, her points of reference were pre-war. She had never thought of it like that before.

He didn't ask to meet Dilys and Geoff and that suited her because she preferred to keep him separate, postponing, for as long as possible, building herself another replica of home, with all the old difficulties creeping up the walls like rising damp. Rob and Ella kept quiet about him too. Rob liked Felpo but he wasn't good at talking to Dilys on the telephone. He only uttered single words. Ella pretended Felpo didn't exist. Occasionally she challenged him with rude questions which he didn't rise to. Then she remembered he didn't exist and reverted to ignoring him. She wouldn't have wasted her breath mentioning him to the grandparents. So the moment to announce that he had come to live with them passed. It never had been the right moment.

Jo heard the door open. There was a pause while someone stood and looked at her. Then Dilys said, 'Aren't you so well, dear?'

'I'm all right,' Jo said, getting up from the floor. 'It was stuffy in here. What time is it?'

'Ten. You've had a good long sleep. Are you sure you're not going down with something?

'Yes. I'm sure. Please don't worry about me,' Jo said.

'You're not depressed, are you? That's a terrible thing.' Jo shook her head.

'I'll get you a dressing gown from upstairs,' Dilys said.

'I don't need one. It's summer.'

Dilys moved the pillow from the sofa on to an armchair and began to fold up the sheet.

'Don't do that now, Gran. I'll do it later. Let's go and have some tea.'

Dilys finished her folding and they walked along the passage to the kitchen. All the noises were outside. The house felt quiet.

'Where is everyone?' Jo said.

'Gone to the shops and to do this and that. Forget about them. It will do you good to have a rest,' Dilys said.

'Is Annie all right?'

'Perfect,' said Dilys. 'She came looking for you but I stopped her. Rob gave her her breakfast. Then they both went out with their grandad. Annie walked. She's getting too big for that pushchair. It'll make her lazy.' Dilys nodded at the teapot and the tea caddy. 'You know where everything is, don't you? I'll let you get on with it.'

Dilys pulled out a chair and sat down. 'I didn't like to ask any questions yesterday, darling. I could see you needed time to settle.'

Jo slowly filled the kettle, her back to the room. She left the tap on a quarter turn, and the water took a long time to get to the top.

'All that luggage you brought with you,' Dilys said.

'I know, Gran.'

Jo still didn't turn round. Water was coming out of the kettle spout. She had overfilled it. She tipped some water out, mopped up the front of the sink unit, then stood the kettle on its stand and switched it on.

'You don't usually bring so much,' Dilys said.

'I know,' she said. 'I understand what you're asking. I don't really have an answer. I might not be going back. I don't know. It would be better if I were someone different. I'd manage better.'

Dilys nodded. Jo waited for the water to boil, then filled the teapot and brought it across. There were two cups and saucers and the biscuit tin waiting on the table. Dilys must have set them out earlier.

'I tried that,' said Dilys, after the pause.

'Tried what?' Jo asked.

'Changing myself,' said Dilys. 'I looked through the hymn writers at the back of the Congregational Hymn Book, not the ones who wrote the tunes. They were men. Settled on Eliza Cross. I thought the world was ready for Eliza Cross. Mother found the little notes and things I'd written. "What's this Eliza Cross?" she said. I wasn't pleased, but after a while she got it out of me. "Well," she said, "I know why you chose that name. It's because you are cross." I cried my eyes out. Mother was like that; a reason for everything, everything cut and dried.'

She paused. She hoped her granddaughter would say that she, Dilys, wasn't like that, but Jo didn't. Dilys carried on as if she had done.

'I made up my mind to be different. I was at the wrong end of her tongue too often not to know about it. Funny, you know, I can still remember how I felt. I'd gone to so much trouble to choose that name.'

Jo had heard the story before, though not for a few years. So her grandmother had tried to be different once too — she'd forgotten that.

73

'Do you think you might try to find a job here?' Dilys said.

'Maybe. I don't know.'

'You'll be lucky to find anything as convenient as Lois Lucas.'

'I know. The big ones will be off my hands before too long. But Annie's so little.'

'You don't regret it, do you?'

'What?'

'Having Annie.'

Jo hesitated.

'I mean, I know you didn't get what you wanted,' Dilys said.

'What did I want?'

Dilys stopped. She was choosing her words.

'What did I want?'

'Well, to keep the family together.'

'Annie was a mistake. I've told you before.'

Dilys shook her head. 'Babies are always welcome when they arrive.'

She meant it too. Jo's own welcome had never been in doubt, in spite of the shock and upheaval.

'An accident then, if that sounds better,' Jo said. She could tell as soon as she spoke that the word was as cheerless. 'He didn't stay, anyway. You're right about that.'

'And what was *she* thinking of? That woman?'

Jo didn't reply. Dilys was stuck with an out of date story. She was looking for a man to blame and having failed to unearth one had fallen back on Peter. Dissolution of marriage was, to her, like a fatal illness. You were unlucky to be visited by it, but the way you'd chosen to live your life made you prone. That anyone could still be alive on the far side astonished Dilys. She and Geoff had worried about her and the children. They had been kind, but Jo had had to carry their kindness as an extra weight, in a container that was already full. The feeling that she, not Peter, had been the less predictable of the two of them had kept her going. Let him play house all over again. She had been the one living on the edge. Her grandparents had expected her to be part of the old family again – in attitude, if not in reality. But she hadn't wanted a refuge. It would have been easy enough to make one; with children it was already half-built. She had known women whose husbands had gone, who had carried on building upwards, leaving a window for the sad and lonely and, with any luck, the man himself to look into and feel left out. But drawing strength from her own rockiness – she couldn't have expected Dilys and Geoff to understand that. Trevor had been more help. He hadn't asked questions. He had sat her in one of the plush chairs, put a glass of red wine in her hand, tuned in to bright chat on the radio and carried on as usual. He had once said that his work triangle was the shop and The Dog and she had imagined the missing part as the sky above, or the air in between, because there was something expansive about Trevor. He didn't fuss in the way other people did. He never had done. She had been able to rely on him for weightless sympathy.

She could see Peter now, awkward by the bed in the maternity ward. He went away for a couple of hours after Annie was born and came back again. She knew immediately that it was different from the earlier births, that he stood in a different relation to her. He looked like Rob, hardly older, just as dependable, but self-conscious, neuter, no longer connected. She was relieved when he vanished down the hospital corridor, leaving her to bury herself under the cotton cellulose blanket and float back up into a patch of light somewhere over the bed and the cot. She liked it up there. Afterwards, once she got back home, she argued herself out of the uneasiness, listened to a voice from within, resembling her grandmother's, telling her that women who'd just had babies didn't see straight. She got on with life, incorporating Annie's sleeping and trembly wailing into the existing lack of routine. She tried not to think that she had postponed freedom by ten years at least. She tried not to think about anything. But she wondered where he was when he seemed so late coming home. The unstable, post-natal way of looking at things kept coming back. She found herself adding and subtracting hours and fractions of hours and trying to reach a conclusion. She never worked out Annie's feeds like that. It had been easy enough for him to get the better of her. She'd never been good at counting or taking careful account of things. His carefulness was palpable, becoming more marked by the week, until, by a sleight of hand which still seemed grotesque, he slid from their conventional relationship to a different but equally conventional one and she was the one left looking excitable and unhinged.

Tara. She had got used to the name now, though she never used it in her grandparents' house. He had met her at work – the pharmaceutical company that had brought them to Kent in the first place. He had mentioned chemistry, or maybe electricity. Something boring. She couldn't remember now.

Dilys looked at the clock. 'The man was coming over to service the boiler this afternoon.'

Jo said, 'So what time is he coming?'

'I put him off. He comes every August. The same man. A Mr Chambers.'

Jo took a deep breath. 'Is there anything you'd like me to do for you while I'm here?' she said.

She glanced up at the high shelf that ran along the chimney-breast. It was overfull and the pale crockery looked dusty. 'I could get on the steps for you. Wash the china,' she said.

'No,' Dilys said. 'Your grandfather and I can still manage. Thank you very much.'

76

3

As soon as Rob set foot in the house he said he wanted to go out again. He seemed to have forgotten it was lunchtime. He mumbled about having seen something that he wanted in a shop. Dilys asked Geoff what it was. Geoff said he had no idea; it was news to him. Jo could see this running on and agreed to go back with Rob in the afternoon. So Rob calmed down and digested the food Dilys had prepared. Scotch eggs, lettuce and beetroot followed by the remains of the apple pie, with ice cream this time. Geoff looked puzzled. He said he'd thought they'd all had a pleasant time together in the precinct. Annie had liked the water feature.

Once they had washed up and *Any Questions* was over, Dilys and Geoff sat down in the front room with a book and the newspaper and a biro for the crossword. The day had distinct parts to it. Jo, Rob and Annie went out. They walked down the street towards the main road where the buses passed. Jo said nothing until they drew level with the house two down from Geoff and Dilys's. The holding back was a habit from her childhood. This was the place where she used to start significant conversation with her friends, or allow reverie to begin. The house was different from the others, flat-fronted, having lost its bay in the Blitz. She had puzzled over it as a child and couldn't understand how, when rebuilding it, the Government had allowed it to look so different. Sixty years on, the bricks that had been used still looked raw and new. They had hardly weathered at all.

'So what's all this about?' Jo said. 'Grandad didn't know what you were on about. And honestly, if you're going to lie, learn to do it properly. It's no good being vague. Black and white trainers you should have said, or a Millwall T-shirt.'

'But I don't want them,' said Rob.

'Walk straight,' Jo said. 'You keep bumping into the buggy.'

They got to the end of the street and Jo turned right along the main road past the Baptist chapel and the straggle of businesses that changed hands between one visit and the next. Nail beauticians and dubious jewellers who offered cash for gold. They altered the signage but couldn't afford to re-paint. Only the dry cleaner had lasted.

'Why are we going here, Mum? It's not the way.'

'We're not carrying out this pantomime to the last detail, looking in an invisible shop for an invisible special offer. We'll have a walk now we're out. Go and have a look at the Thames.'

'But what shall we say to Gran and Grandad when we get back?'

'Grow up,' she said.

Jo knew she was snapping, but it was safe. She wasn't able to risk kindness.

They crossed the road at the traffic lights and turned immediately down a narrow passage. They moved abruptly out of the sunshine and into black shadow doubly cast by a disused industrial building on one side and a high wall topped with corrugated-iron sheets on the other.

'There isn't a phone box down here,' Rob said.

Jo stopped. After the brightness it was difficult to see anything. She looked about. No, there wasn't a phone box.

'You should have let us have mobiles,' he said.

'Let doesn't come into it. When you can pay your bills you can have one. Anyway, Ella would keep hers switched off.'

'You should find out if Ella's all right, though,' he said.

'How do you suggest I do that?'

'Call someone.'

'I told you yesterday, she'll be fine. She goes her own way when it suits her, which is most of the time. Why is this different?'

'Just check. See if she's gone back there.'

'Back where?'

'Home. See if she's there. Just see.'

'She'll go to your dad's if she can't think of anything better,' Jo said.

'Call him, then. Please, Mum.'

There were three notices on the wall behind Rob, each a different shape and in different lettering. Keep Out. Beware of the Dog. Warning, these Premises are guarded by a Patrol Room 24 hour manned. Jo read them in turn. They must have started with the simple one, then when they got trouble added the dog and when they got more trouble added the patrol room. So many defences for one tinny scrap yard. They cancelled each other out. The place was a pushover.

'I'm tired,' she said. 'We'll show Annie the Thames. Then we'll turn back.'

She could have spent the rest of her life standing in that dark place and she wouldn't have cared. She forced herself to walk. Rob dragged along behind.

She remembered how she had been at the age of twenty shortly before she got married and left home. In a kind of fog – though she hadn't realised at the time. She saw herself in a clingy blue dress with a slit at the side getting into Peter's car. Too tight, they had said.

She hadn't been her best at twenty. Escaping from Dilys and Geoff, not being Dilys and Geoff, had seemed enough. She had climbed what she had imagined was out of reach and had never noticed a mist come down. As a child, she had thought longer and more clearly. She had had plenty to think

79

about – her mother, who had got clean away by dying; her grandma, who was a pervading presence. She had looked eagerly for well-defined people in between – people who occupied a specific space in reality and no more. There had been a woman in their road she'd thought about. She and Rob had passed the house as they walked to the main road. Mrs Delamare. Jo had never known her first name. She wasn't a neighbour that Dilys passed the time of day with. Dilys used to speak about her behaviour. This was to Geoff, of course, not to her young granddaughter. Overhearing her was Jo's first intimation that grown-ups behaved. She had been surprised. She'd thought behaviour was confined to children. Mrs Delamare's husband had left – gone, up or down the line, they'd said. Whether this was a euphemism, or he worked for the railway, Jo hadn't known. Asking often failed to clarify this sort of thing. The woman had had pretty hair, which Dilys used to say was dyed, though it probably wasn't. Soft and reddish it was, plenty of it. Not long after Mr Delamare's disappearance, a man had started to visit, arriving in the early evening, setting out in the morning. He had had a key, but he had never put the dustbin out on Sunday night. He used not to be there then, or on Friday or Saturday nights. Jo didn't think she had romanticised the love affair, though she had liked the way he locked his hands round the back of Mrs Delamare's waist to pull her to him and kiss her. Women's waists used to be smaller then. They were still encircling them with tape measures. Sexier than standing on the scales. What had interested Jo were the woman's solitary weekends. Mrs Delamare had worn old clothes and had looked serene, sitting on the front step on warm days. She used to come out in the morning in a frayed green kimono, not to grab the pint of milk but to smoke half a cigarette and blow smoke rings into the sky. Then late in the evening she did her cleaning and ironing with the lights on and the curtains wide open. She had treated her front yard and the road outside as unselfconsciously as the other neighbours did the back. The man used to come in that way. Jo had thought that was perhaps why she liked being out there.

No one else had done these things. And, apart from the man, there had been no visitors: no elderly relations, no Sunday lunches that made the whole street smell of burnt dripping and gravy. Jo used to try to work out how such a life could be arrived at. She had seen that it wasn't going to be easy. She had been very young, but she had understood the woman's peacefulness and where it came from. It had already been in her bones, waiting.

She had taken Felpo home after they had made love for the first time. He had moved in that same afternoon. It had been easy. He was four years younger than she was. He'd been a hospital porter and a barman and a courier. He'd lived in rented rooms and other people's flats and once in a loft over an egg-packing shed in Hertfordshire. He'd broken his arm jumping off a garage roof when he was ten and had salmonella from eating tuna from a dented tin. He ate everything apart from coleslaw. Jo had found out that much on their way from Lois Lucas & Son to the flat but she hadn't, at that stage, known anything else about him, neither the form-filling stuff, nor the tired particulars which are squeezed out of the question, What sort of person is he? These things explain nothing. Some people, although new to you, come with labels attached. They stick them on themselves, as large as sandwich boards sometimes. They want you to know who they are and where they come from. He wasn't like that.

She had often thought how it would be with another kind of man. Several other kinds of men, but all rolled up into the same difficulty. She had had a few propositions made to her since she had stopped being married. Not blatantly adulterous, which is what she would have expected, just weird. There was the man on the beach who beckoned and murmured 'Lubberly lubberly'. And the man who came to sit opposite her and Annie in Bettine's café and offered her a tot of rum in her cup of tea. Then there were others who were less gross but who still carried desperation around with them like a mobile phone that was tucked away but inevitably started ringing. She hadn't seen these overtures as opportunities. They made her fed up. The easiness of something better she had known about, but only deep down, she hadn't been able to retrieve it. Different from the off-putting stories she could elaborate on indefinitely. The embarrassment of introducing a new man to Ella and Rob.

This is John, a straightforward, self-conscious, not entirely smitten bloke, who's just popped in for a drink/cup of tea/pee.

Here's John again. He's come for supper. Oh, a bottle of wine, how thoughtful.

Here's John. We're off to the pub. Could you baby-sit for an hour or so? (The presuming hand laid on her to guide her out of her own house.)

Here's John. He thinks he might be over the limit, so he's staying. (The presuming hand laid on her to guide her back in again.)

Felpo had his feet in between hers, while John was still checking to see if he'd locked the car. He made her brave. Perhaps she had already become brave. He arrived at the moment she was independent enough from her old married self to be able to pull it off.

Jo remembered the way he looked at her before he left the shop to deliver the leaflets for the Fun Run lady. It might have meant something. The sense was usually accurate; it just never guaranteed future events. Annie asked her about the man and the invisible tiger. She asked repeatedly. Jo thought about him as she talked but the thoughts didn't fit the words; the picture in her mind was entirely different. She supposed that that was what conscience was for, to stop such flawed conjunctions. She had never got the hang of any of that: peering into her own mind with the part of herself that was a cut above the ordinary, disapproving of what she saw and zapping it. The next stage would be to approve and admire the view. That couldn't be right. Ella said that if she talked about every sad idiot who came into Lois Lucas's, they'd be there all night. Jo hadn't expected to see him again but the following week when she was on her own in the shop he came back.

She was drawing, resting the piece of paper on an old atlas. She often drew when there weren't any customers. She heard the door of the shop open and shoved the paper out of sight under a newspaper. He came across to where she was sitting and put both hands on the table. Jo hadn't imagined him so near so soon, whatever she had got them doing later. She felt the solidity of it. She hadn't thought of him as possessing any. She looked up and he was standing there with the old-leaves smell of hemp and damp hair, which she remembered, hanging about him. He was wearing the same black coat and had the same woven bag slung over his shoulder. She knew he had come to find her. He didn't pretend he was collecting seventies vinyls, or old clock parts. Jo drew the blind and put the closed sign up. Two women were standing outside, one right up against the glass, pointing out an embroidered fire screen to the other. She looked startled when Jo erased her. The last Jo saw of her face was her mouth, thin lipsticked lines opening. There was a strand of dull light at the bottom of the blind but it went nowhere. She and Felpo sat close together on one of the tip-up seats. They pretended they were in the back row of the Ramsgate Winter Garden. He took her hand in his. They stayed true to the time and place for a while, making the moves authentic to darkened halls. They whispered and tried to keep quiet. Then the others left silently, the audience and the players, the band leader and the girl with the ices and boxes of chocolate assortments. They left and they never came back. The smell of tobacco smoked long ago was embedded in the plush. Jo had never noticed before.

83

'That's why it had to shut,' he said to her afterwards. 'They don't like that kind of behaviour in the Winter Garden.'

They went back home. The children were in the kitchen.

'I've seen you before, haven't I?' Ella said.

'Last week,' Felpo said.

Rob said, 'You're late, Mum.'

'No later than usual,' she said.

'Your mum's been putting life back into seaside theatre,' Felpo said. 'You need to watch her.'

'What do you mean?' Rob said, disbelieving. 'She's never done anything like that.'

Felpo looked taken aback and then laughed. Ella said that there wasn't a theatre and asked where Trevor had been. Jo said he was asleep upstairs. Ella said, 'So he *was* there then.' Jo agreed that he had been and then felt uncomfortable about it for the first time, though there was no reason to be. There always was someone in a room nearby. Ella went to great lengths to make herself a sandwich; slicing the bread as though it were a side of bacon, boiling eggs so fiercely that they knocked against the sides of the pan, plunging tomatoes in hot water before skinning them and chopping them up. They all stood around and watched her assemble this monument, douse it with parsley and pepper, put it on a plate and carry it out of the room. Jo said that they'd all better have something to eat; it was nearly half past two. She made some food but it wasn't as magnificent.

It was a shock for Jo to come out of the alley and be faced with sparkling water that lapped the footpath and stretched across to the Isle of Dogs.

'It's better than the sea,' Rob said. 'Isn't it, Mum?'

'It almost is the sea,' Jo said. 'Smell it.'

The Thames was wide in this part of London. The pleasure boats and the police launches, even big industrial barges, had the freedom of the water. A few summers ago they'd seen a cruise ship. It had filled the river, but there had still been room for other vessels to pass.

A boy of about Rob's age clattered by on a skateboard. He was competent. Once he'd passed he looked back over his shoulder at them both, while still moving. His head stayed swivelled and the board carried him away. Rob breathed in, but he seemed to have forgotten why he was doing it. He moved away from the rail where he'd been leaning.

'What are you staring at?' Jo asked.

'You don't look well,' Rob said.

'It's because it's so bright. You see all the faults.'

She ran a finger down the curve of her face.

'Don't keep looking at it,' she said. 'It's getting better.'

'How do you know?'

'It itches, that means it's starting to heal. Mr Chambers probably wouldn't even have noticed.'

'Mr Chambers. Who are you talking about, Mum?'

'I don't know. Someone who was supposed to be doing some work for Gran and Grandad, this afternoon. He wasn't allowed to see me. Stupid. He's probably got several daughters with messed-up faces.'

'Why don't you sit in the sun, Mum, and I'll walk along to those wooden steps that go into the river? I'll take Annie if you like. I won't let her fall in.'

'I think she's asleep. Yes, she is. You can leave her. Are you wearing a watch? Be back in an hour,' she said.

He set off, half running, glad to get away from her, she thought. How long the day was. The same from hour to hour. Like a ringing in the ears, on and on. Sometimes there was a buzz of interference, which distracted her, but never silence. She sat there on a low wall, facing the water, and nothing got better, though it was the most beautiful day. The far side of the Thames was at a satisfying distance for the eyes. Jo could see every building without straining, clean-edged and calm in the sunshine. The view stretched away between two far-apart bends in the river. She had to turn her head, one way, then the other, to take it all in. If the last six months could be measured along the same stretch it wouldn't extend so far. No more than a few hundred metres – say from the new development with its glassy penthouse to the red brick dome of the Greenwich foot tunnel entrance. No further. It had all been as quick as a story told to Annie and with its core somewhere apart – a heart, inside an egg, inside a bird floating on water. She didn't have a single photograph. Something to carry about with her.

4

Walking away from the supermarket, Ella thought that her gran might be right about Saturday shoppers. Everyone in there – even the ones who weren't talking to themselves or communing with the pet food – seemed to her to have some major personality defect. The human equivalent of wonky trolley wheels. Dilys would only shop on weekday mornings in the company of like-minded people. That was her phrase. She wasn't snobbish, her gran. She believed she was at one with the decent people of Great Britain – who were probably more than half the population – and that they were recognisable by wearing macs in wet weather and not eating anything in the street other than a boiled sweet or an extra-strong mint. Some of them could be black. That wasn't a problem.

Ella was in a no-man's land of shrubby plants and cobbled paths that linked the trading estate with the main road. Purple and lime-green foliage alternated with pink cobbles. The Council had hoped to make a park of the area but it hadn't worked out. She walked along, pausing to bite into the triangular see-through container with her front teeth to get at her sandwich. Smoked salmon and lettuce, it was, since her dad had been paying. The path kept making right angles and she wondered if she'd end up back at the supermarket. There wasn't even a bin. She didn't want the inside of her bag to smell so she jammed the plastic packaging deep into a purple hedge and carried on eating.

She had left Peter and Tara to get on with their day. They hoovered up the hours. She found it tiring to be with them. She found everything tiring, having got up so early. It was well known that people her age needed more sleep. They needed to lose consciousness for hours on end to recover from stopping being funny and sweet like Annie and turning into the beings that made the world what it was. They had this weird energy, the adults she knew. It seemed to come from changing partners. Her gran was quick on the draw, but, together, Dilys and Geoff were nice and slow. The longer people stayed with each other, the slower they got. Old married couples went to sleep when there was nothing to do.

She had come home one day and found Felpo dancing, swaying round the kitchen to some swooshing ballad. It was the sort of thing that got played in the reception area at the swimming baths, only the attendant lady had the sense to turn the volume down. Jo was out of breath so Ella knew that she had been joining in, though luckily she didn't get to see her arms flailing and her knees at funny angles. Jo said she'd found the record in Trevor's box of old singles. Felpo stopped dancing and hugged Jo. He said she had no need to make excuses. It was a classic. They had both laughed then as if it was the funniest remark in the world.

The flat always looked and smelled quite different with him in it, even when he wasn't dancing. He left those wiry jerseys he wore hanging over the backs of chairs and his shoes by the door just where she tripped over them. He only wore shoes outside. She could never forget he was there. Sometimes he would just sit, very still, for an hour at a time, just dropping the odd word to Jo – stroking Jo's knee if she were nearby – pretending to meditate. Ella asked him what he was doing and that's what he said – meditating. She wished she hadn't bothered. She could tell that he was thinking – the same as everybody else.

The path came to a sudden end with a pedestrian safety

barrier at waist height and cars passing at speed on a main road with no pavement. Ella pulled herself up short. She hadn't meant to let Felpo come into her mind. It was Tara's fault. She always seemed to bring Felpo into the conversation. She was fascinated by him.

No planning had gone into this path. If she had been a dog she would have been run over. She launched herself alongside the traffic, holding her arms away from her body in order to cool off – giving any driver, who slightly misjudged, the opportunity to shave a slice off her.

'You look better,' said Vince.

'Thanks,' said Ella.

She moved from mood to mood, but the changes didn't depend on where she was or whom she was with. She had so few places to go and, in spite of the long walks and bus rides between, it took too little time to get from one to the next. Now she was back in Vince's house and it was only twenty-four hours since she had last been there. She was damp from the shower. She had wet hair and was wearing borrowed clothes, Vince's. His mother was shorter than she was, he said. Her clothes wouldn't fit. Ella thought she and Lauren were much the same height and guessed that Vince hadn't wanted her to look in his mother's wardrobe. She wasn't going to argue – she didn't want to wear anything of Lauren's.

'I was going to have a bath round at Dad's, but it didn't work out,' Ella said. 'They're on some sort of automatic timer; if you miss your slot, that's it. I went round the supermarket with them instead.'

'Nice one,' said Vince. 'I haven't done that for years. I should try it. Isn't there a nudist evening?'

'That's Hastings. They wouldn't let you on the bus.'

Vince nodded, accepting this.

'He really put pressure on me to stay longer,' Ella said. 'He wanted me to have some upmarket pub lunch. He always does that.'

'You look better than me in those shorts. You can keep them if you want,' Vince said.

'No, it's all right,' Ella said.

She went over to the window of the living room and stared out. The pigeons were still there, hunched up and almost black in colour, lined up in the same formation.

'Dad hangs on to the trolley with this funny look on his face,' Ella said, 'as if he's on a fairground ride and supposed to be enjoying it. Tara does all the choosing. Anything he sticks in, she whips out again. We get to the check-out. She finds this cheddar cheese that got away. She picks it up, like this, as if she's found something truly disgusting and balances it on the pile of cooking magazines. Dad sort of smiles and pretends none of it's happening.'

'They're probably like that in bed,' Vince said.

'They're supposed to be in love,' Ella said. 'That's why he left Mum.'

'It's their age,' Vince said. 'All that middle bit. How do you get through it?'

'Don't ask me.'

Ella turned round to face the room, but she didn't sit down.

'It's like the afternoon,' said Vince. 'No point to it. Just there to join up the morning and the evening. I mean, the morning's easy, isn't it, you can deal with it, unless you're hung-over or something? But the afternoon. What a waste of time. Think of school. The radiators and the smell really getting going, everyone yawning, teachers with bits of bacon sandwich stuck in their teeth.'

Ella didn't want to think of school. The place had no reality without its counterpart – home. And for the moment she had no home. She remembered the previous September after the holidays. She saw herself leaning against the high wire fence with a group of sun-tanned girls – getting to know them again. The weather had been hot, the same as it was now. The teachers were wearing what they had worn in July and the kids' discarded jerseys and blazers were piled up in heaps.

'People our parents' age don't have birth or death to gee them up,' Vince said. 'They need something in the middle of life. I'd give them an ordeal.'

'Like what?' Ella said.

'They'd have to go through this tunnel,' he said.

'They're always going in tunnels,' she said.

Vince ignored her. 'It would be lined with mirrors. On a particular day they'd be shown the entrance – they'd walk and walk. It would go on for miles.'

'What good would that do?' Ella said.

'They'd get sick of the sight of themselves. Reality would kick in.'

'It wouldn't work,' Ella said. 'They'd probably just plan their next year's holiday.'

'It's a cool idea, you have to admit. It would make great TV. Some people would go mad,' Vince said.

'Would they have to talk?'

'Yes, of course they'd talk. They'd sort of ramble on.'

'It wouldn't change anything. Afterwards they'd just carry on being the selves they always pretend to be,' Ella said.

'Not necessarily,' Vince said.

'I hope you'll give them a nice packed lunch,' she said.

Vince had his back to the sofa and his legs stretched out in front of him. He leant to one side and, with his two forefingers, dragged two parallel lines across the pile of the carpet.

'So, where did you spend the night?' he said.

'At Lois Lucas & Son's. It's this kind of antique shop where Mum works. I work there sometimes at the week-ends. I've got a key.'

'Antique,' said Vince. 'Was that all right?'

'Not bad,' said Ella. 'I did get some sleep.'

'I couldn't stand that – waking up every fifteen minutes with the chiming clocks.'

He started to intone a version of the Westminster chimes.

'You've got to be joking. Trevor doesn't have those sorts of clock,' she said, interrupting.

'Trevor?' he said.

'He's the owner. He lives over the shop.'

'He's gay, is he?'

'Not as far as I know,' Ella said.

'Oh,' Vince said.

He pushed against the waste-paper basket with his right foot. The basket fell over and the contents tipped on the floor: a clutch of flyers from a pizza delivery company, yesterday's newspaper, a couple of envelopes, a brown apple core.

'Aren't you going to pick them up?' Ella said.

'No,' said Vince.

He tore off a corner of newspaper and wrapped the apple core in it.

'So you know Trevor pretty well?' he said.

'No,' Ella said. 'I was downstairs. I don't know whether he was upstairs or not. He might have been.'

Vince made a graded pile of the rubbish, ending with the wrapped core that sat on top like a paperweight.

She knew what he was thinking. He was as transparent as a clean pond. All those tiddlers in his mind coming to life. She raised her eyebrows and looked indifferent.

'You'll stay there forever, will you?' he said. 'Gathering dust, as my nan says.'

'Is she the one who shifts the furniture?'

'Yes. Not that it has much chance to gather anything. If Ray won't go round, she asks anyone in, complete strangers.'

'Could I move in with her?' asked Ella. 'I'd like to give her a hand. I move stuff round my room too. I'm strong. I won the triathlon.'

'No you didn't,' said Vince. 'Lisa Summers did. Nan's

barmy. I mean it. She thinks things are behind the cupboards. She's not happy unless it's all on the move and the things can't hide. Her sister's already in hospital with it. Nan visits her every Friday.'

'Does she go on the bus?'

'What a stupid question,' said Vince. 'No, she drives a Ferrari.'

'I think I saw her.'

'Where?'

'On the bus. Yesterday.'

'What were you doing on it?'

'Nothing particular,' said Ella. 'Forget it.'

Vince gave her a cool look. She could see him thinking she was an odd girl and that she was even odder than he had thought. They had known each other for a couple of years now, though they were never in the same classes because he was younger. She had noticed him when he first joined the school because he didn't look like a new boy. He was taller than the others and his blazer was a few shades lighter. She'd never liked to ask him whether it had belonged to his brother and faded with age or been put through a hot wash.

Ella moved away from the window and lay down flat on the floor.

'Are you feeling ill?' Vince said.

She shook her head. 'Put some music on,' she said.

'What do you want?'

'Anything. You choose.'

'This is all Ray's stuff.'

Vince got up and walked across the room. He stared at the edges of the CDs, stacked in a tower.

'You wouldn't like any of this. We could go upstairs to my room. We can smoke up there. My brother doesn't mind,' Vince said.

'It's all right,' Ella said.

'What do you want to do then?' he said.

'I don't know. Have you got any animals? We could walk your dog.'

'I don't have a dog. You'd have seen it by now. Dogs always say hi. Do you have one, then?'

'No. We're not allowed pets,' she said. 'Mum bought her boyfriend a goldfish for his birthday. She never buys *us* anything living. She made him a sticky chocolate cake for breakfast. Then they went out together to buy some weed from the garden centre.'

'Did he want a goldfish?' Vince said.

'I don't think so. She asked him if it reminded him of the one he'd had when he was little.'

'Did it?'

'He said it was much prettier. He always spouts crap. How could he remember?'

They heard the door click. Ella rolled on to her stomach and lifted her head to see who it was.

Ray was hobbling into the room with a towel round his waist. He lowered himself on to the sofa.

'I told you, you didn't want to sleep on there,' Vince said.

'What's that?' asked Ray.

'Isn't the treatment working?' Ella said.

'Too bloody right, it's not,' Ray said.

'You should try sleeping on pebbles, like Ella,' said Vince. 'Good for the muscles.'

'I didn't,' Ella said. 'I just told you.'

'Girl's got more sense,' said Ray. 'Sort of crackpot idea you'd come up with. So what are you two doing for the rest of the day?' he asked, with his eyes shut.

They could hear the washing machine, with Ella's clothes inside, humming drowsily through the wall.

'Nothing, as far as I know,' said Vince.

Ray snorted. 'I saw you'd taken that hat off. I thought it meant you were going somewhere.'

5

Jo walked back from the river with Rob in near silence. She asked him if he'd seen any interesting boats or if he had bought himself some sweets. She sounded like Geoff – but not as nice. She had lost the knack of talking. Annie woke up and ran in and out of other people's front gates.

'Wait, wait,' she said.

And when they turned round she was holding a fat orange dahlia in her hands – just the bloom, without a stem.

'Are you letting her do that?' Rob said.

Geoff was looking out for them as they walked up the path but Jo smiled a few seconds too late. He had already turned away to open the door. Dilys came up behind him in the hall and greeted them by saying that they were later than she and Geoff had expected. The clock on the wall said five o'clock. A blameless time, Jo would have thought. Dilys asked if Rob had found what he wanted at the shops. Both Jo and Rob had forgotten that this was the reason for going out and said yes and no simultaneously. Jo went up to the bathroom, splashed her face with cold water and washed her hands, turning the pink scented soap over and over under the running tap. She could hear Geoff setting out cups and saucers on a tray in the kitchen, then the chinking they made as he carried them to the front room. Rob had wanted her to say something. He would have known how to stop her from talking, if she'd worried or embarrassed him, but he had no way of making her start. He had taken to Felpo. She had been glad; though she hadn't always wanted a large boy accompanying them. He would miss him, she thought. The tiny strips of sticking plaster on her cheek were beginning to loosen. She picked one off and looked at herself in the mirror. The wound was mending. There was no fresh blood. She tried another one, then a couple more. The last few were slightly stickier but she eased them off. Then she dabbed around with damp cotton wool. She stayed in front of the basin until her face had dried. When she went downstairs again they were all drinking tea and watching the news. The back window was open and through it she could hear the screams and laughter of kids playing in the next street and the retreating tune of an ice-cream van. Santa Lucia. It was a tune that went round in a circle – like all the worst tunes. Dilys had never allowed her to buy a cone from the van. She said the ice cream was made in a plastic bag in the man's back garden and would make her sick. She had made Jo go to the newsagent and get a wrapped slab from the deep freeze that was then jammed in a cornet or slapped between wafers.

She wondered if Dilys and Geoff had been saying things about her while they were out. She had always hated cropping up in conversations she wasn't taking part in. As a child, she had spent a lot of time hanging around half listening, hoping she wouldn't hear her name mentioned but determined to be within hearing distance if it were. Overhearing Dilys talk about her had been like sniffing neat peppermint oil. She hadn't recognised herself, or at least, she hadn't recognised the fixedness of it. She had felt fluid, unmade, but had discovered that not only was she these things her grandmother said she was – dreamy, careless, clever, too clever by half – as surely as her eyes were a particular colour, but that she did what she did because of them. They were the explanation. For instance, Jo had thought that she had failed to open her mouth in the presence of Dilys's cousin, Frank (visiting from Australia), because he'd smelled of ear wax and had shoes with the eyelets so placed that they looked like small dangerous animals. But she had learned that it was because she was shy. And this single word, like other single words that described her, hadn't floated free; it had been weighted down at its corners with causes and consequences. *It would be a handicap until she grew out of it. It came from Dilys's middle sister, Jean. It had a good side, which was that she could be depended on not to show off in company but to be quiet and lose herself in a book.* It hadn't stopped her from being interested in strangers until they spoke to her, which, of course, they did, as she'd looked at them with such interest. Geoff, disappointingly, had agreed with Dilys, though he'd called it unforthcoming. It had been one way to acquire vocabulary. She hadn't liked other people speaking about her mother either – what had happened to her. She had found it insulting. She felt protective towards the young woman whose old toys she played with and whose school projects were still in a cupboard upstairs.

She tried not to talk about Ella, Rob or Annie out of their hearing. Particularly the older two. Both their father and their great grandmother would, she knew, have liked to hear more anecdotes. They didn't live with the children and wanted to feel included. Occasionally she failed: she set sail down the telephone on paper boats – her daughter the Drama Queen, her son the Conformist. The compliant applause fluttered back down the wire. But her children didn't need to be explained. They were strong. Explanation broke on the strength of them. She hadn't been as invincible.

Jo sat down and picked up the only full cup that was left on the tray. She tried to focus on the scene before her. Airport chaos. People sitting on luggage. A little girl missing from a camp site in Cumbria. The newscaster's voice seemed to come back louder with each new item. Jo watched but couldn't, at the end, have said what had been happening.

There was always a sequence of sorts. Hopes fade, feared dead, found dead. She couldn't recall which stage had been reached. Once the weather forecast was over Geoff turned the volume down to a murmur. Rob leant forward in order to carry on listening. Annie drew shapes in the air with her finger.

'Did you bring me any books?' Dilys said.

'No. Sorry, Gran. Not this time,' Jo said.

'I expect you had too much to think about,' Dilys said. 'The print was too small.'

Trevor acquired books in job lots from his ladies along with the rest of the rubbish. She usually picked out one or two for Dilys. The latest batch had come from a kleptomaniac who had never taken back library books. They had become non-returnable, the library in question having shut for good ten years ago. No one wanted to buy them. They had shrunk inside their covers like old people who have shrivelled, but carry on wearing their clothes of plumper days. The Sellotape holding them together was crisp with age. It was probably true that the print was too small. But she hadn't bothered to look.

Geoff got up and looked out of the window.

'Marion's son's car is still there,' he said.

'She'll be glad to have company,' Dilys said. She turned to Jo. 'She had the burglars a week ago. Did I tell you about that?'

'I don't think so,' Jo said.

She moved slightly in the chair to face her grandmother and made herself pay attention. Marion was a comparative newcomer, having moved in since Jo left home. No memories attached to her. She tried to form pictures as Dilys talked, exorbitant pictures that would fill her mind. Marion asleep in her bed, a man climbing over the back fence, a strange hand opening and shutting drawers, the Krugerrand in a felt box that the burglar had turned his nose up at. She had met Marion and liked her, but that didn't make any difference, the images failed to appear. It was like trying to light up a room by striking a dead match. When Dilys paused, Jo forgot to say anything. She looked round, hoping that something on the walls would jog her memory.

'I'm sorry,' she said.

She felt sorry.

Geoff nodded.

Dilys started up again. 'She didn't hear him break in because an early-morning aeroplane flew over the house,' she said.

'Say that again, Gran,' Rob said.

'They start every morning. Four a.m. You can set the clock by them,' Dilys said.

'What's that got to do with it?' Rob said.

'She'd have heard the glass smash otherwise. So she said.'

'But how did Marion know? That's what I mean,' Rob said.

'The first she knew of it was when she came downstairs and felt the draught,' Dilys said.

'Leave it, Rob,' Jo said.

'She thought it might have been the boy who comes door to door selling dusters and gardening gloves who did it. Ridiculous prices he charges,' Dilys said.

'Why pick on him?' Rob said.

'He was very careful,' Dilys said. 'He didn't leave a mess. She was grateful for that.'

'I thought you said he smashed the window,' Rob said. 'You wouldn't call it careful if I smashed a window. Even by mistake.'

'Rob,' Jo said.

'He didn't harm her,' Geoff said. 'That's the main thing.'

'Ella's not nervous, being on her own at night?' Dilys said.

'Not as far as I know,' Jo said. 'She doesn't seem to be nervous of anything.'

'She seems young to me to be left,' Dilys said.

Jo watched as Geoff collected up the cups and carried

them out on the tray. She looked back at the television screen, mottled gold as the sky it reflected. She had only been to see Dilys and Geoff once since March. It had just been for the day. She had gone with Annie, up and down on the usual trains. Felpo had come to meet them at the station. Her grandparents had said how well she looked. Bonny, Geoff had said – and they hadn't asked her why. They weren't like that.

Now another evening stretched ahead. Annie to be put to bed. The table laid. Food prepared. And eaten. No one had mentioned her cheek – the fact that the plasters were off – though they had all had a good look at it.

6

There were still people moseying around Lois Lucas & Son. Most of the shops and tea-rooms had closed so the day-trippers who weren't ready to drive back home wandered the streets. They were relieved to find somewhere to pass the time. Even in fine weather they liked to shop. Trevor generally picked up a bit of trade at the end of the day. He got up from his chair on the pavement and went inside to pour himself another glass of wine. A man and a woman were opening and shutting the doors of the huge mahogany wardrobe, sticking their heads right inside it. Woodworm, he supposed they were looking for. He was fairly certain it was clean, though he hadn't looked too closely. He hoped they wouldn't want the wardrobe. Unless they had come in a decent-sized van that was parked round the corner, they wouldn't be able to have it. He dodged past them into the kitchen. He didn't want them to start asking him questions. Would he deliver it to Bromley, preferably this evening, or, at the latest, first thing tomorrow morning? Would he put it in acid to strip off the varnish? Someone had asked him that once. What did they take him for – even a serial killer wouldn't have an acid bath the size of a small swimming pool. One day he'd just have to set light to all the big pieces. They caused too much aggravation. Sometimes he found a mate with transport to help him out with deliveries, but he couldn't depend on it. Blokes with vehicles over a certain size were a law unto themselves. If he managed to pin them down, he never knew what favour they'd ask in return. He wasn't up for burying asylum seekers who had been accidentally suffocated.

Jo's boyfriend had shifted a hospital bed for him. Delivered it to a couple outside Sittingbourne. He'd been obliging. He did removals – the sort that used to be called light but which as a term had gone, together with the Light Programme. Man with a Van it was now. Trevor had asked if he put No Job Too Small when he advertised. He said he didn't bother with advertising. One thing led to another, he said.

He was a nice enough fellow, the boyfriendo. Sweet pea with Jo. They seemed devoted. People were said to go for the same partner again and again and there was something about him that reminded Trevor of Jo's ex – a touch of the beseeching hound, though the breeds were different. He'd met the ex once or twice when he'd come to pick up the kids from the shop. *She* seemed to think she had branched out a bit and that was what mattered. Amazing that bed had been. He'd regretted accepting it from the widowed headmaster, but the first day he got it in the shop everyone wanted it – he could have sold it several times over. There was no point in asking why. If there was a craze in Kent for playing doctors and patients he didn't want to know about it. Lois had had a bit of an eye for that sort of thing. She read the posh magazines when she got a chance, knew whether chinoiserie or brass was making a comeback. His point was that it was all a mystery – what people wanted.

He skulked in the kitchen until the couple had got out of the wardrobe and left the premises. Then he felt free to come out of hiding. Only a few customers were left now: a woman leafing through old comics, another holding a satin lampshade up to the light as if it were a piece of fine china while her child drummed out a tune on a typewriter. He picked up a shiny teacup and examined the rivets that kept the handle on. Ugly, like metal fillings in teeth. He used to have a chap who could do little jobs like that but his hands got too shaky to carry on working. A lot of the junk had to do with tea and old-fashioned ways of drinking it that had passed away with the original owners. Slop basins, sugar tongs, tea strainers. They weren't fast-moving lines, unless some new illegal use could be found for them. They had that look about them which suggested medicine and decadence. Caught in the street with sugar tongs in your pocket: instant arrest on suspicion.

Eventually the shop emptied. The woman hadn't bought the lampshade but her boy had nicked a peacock feather. He waved it as he went out. Trevor took a couple of notes out of the tin box and locked it again without counting the money. He knew more or less what was there. A sheaf of tenners and fivers. Some loose change. A thirty-quid cheque for the lopsided airing rack. He had Francesca, the new care worker at Borrowdale, to ponder on. She was pretty enough, very pretty, in fact, in an East European sort of way. Different from the usual run. Though there was generally one presentable one per retirement home – usually a temp – who hadn't developed the optimistic facial expressions, or the hands atrophied by germicidal soap and hot water. Francesca had seemed encouragingly depressed by the ambience of Borrowdale, managing to smile at him in a different way from the sombre smile she gave the elderly. Her face was otherwise inexpressive and that, together with the nice bloom to her skin, made him think of an egg in a grey egg box. She had eyebrows that rose and fell like the eyebrows of a sad heroine in a silent film. Past thirty, a moderate showing of low spirits was a good sign, he always thought, promising worldliness and some experience with men. Scope for cheering up in the old style.

They'd had a nice chat over coffee and biscuits in the day lounge with the retired ones splayed out on the sofas. He'd found her voice restful. The way she said Borrowdale, with the accented first syllable and the rr like a cat purring – he kept hoping she'd repeat it. She was homesick, she said. He'd sympathised with that, having never left home himself for longer than a fortnight. When he had asked her what she was doing on Saturday evening she'd told him she was on duty, but that hadn't seemed to worry her and certainly hadn't worried him. They hadn't exactly made a date – but neither had she been actively discouraging. He had written her name in his diary.

He went upstairs to shave and put a comb through his hair, maybe change his shirt. He felt slightly disconnected, almost reflective. It must be the heat, he thought. He opened his bedroom door and surveyed his upstairs arrangements. No one could call them domestic. Even qualified by chaotic or squalid the word had a solidity and cleanliness which shone through. The true junk ended up here, among his socks and wet towels and the Indian take-away packaging with slicks of sauce still clinging to the inside. These were the things that even he knew could never be sold and that would have turned to mush if he had left them in the yard at the back. The stained tea cosies and odd elastic stockings, the cushion covers and net curtains. He never knew whether they were included in the boxes because the clients thought someone would make use of them, or to pad out the breakables. The truss can't have been for that; it was a liability among the sherry glasses. They were on their way to the dump, he said, when Jo asked him what he planned to do with them. She had asked him where it was, the dump – only out of interest, she hadn't been offering to go – and he said he didn't have any idea, he would know it when he got there. She'd said he made it sound like heaven.

His love life was conducted off the premises. A week after his mother died, while the place was still orderly, he'd brought a woman back, but so soon after the cremation, the mood had left him. He'd tried once more a few days later with the same woman, and then with a different one a month or so after that. Nothing doing. He had given up on girlfriends for a while. Then he had met Buffie who was living on a permanent site behind the White Cliffs Country Trail. She hadn't wanted to leave the caravan empty at night. Squatters kept a look-out for empty property, she said. It had been a relief to him that his old form came back. Buffie had sugared off to the Isle of Wight to give seaweed treatments at a beauty salon her friend had opened. But then there had been others. There were always spare women at the seaside. Of course, it wasn't an ideal situation. He found it inconvenient not to wake up at his own place, especially in the winter when he had to turn out in the cold.

Beyond the foreground debris he could see the bed, a collapsed heap of sheeting and discoloured ribbon-edged blankets, which, because not tucked in, revealed the mattress with its ticking cover and felted buttons. It looked pretty rancid. He sniffed, in case it also ponged, and then shook his head at his own disquiet, as over a good pair of shoes that had developed a silly squeak. He focused on his essentials, plainly visible in the conventional place on top of the dressing table: brush, comb, nail scissors, electric shaver. This was the only square foot that was uncorrupted. He went across to pick up the shaver and the comb and left the room. There wasn't much else to the building. A few uneven steps led down to the landing and up again to the low cupboard in the roof space and the bathroom that smelled of river mud when the window was shut. He went up the steps, tripping over the top one in the darkness. The bathroom was rank – the fittings scabbed over with green-streaked lime scale. Jo never went there, he noticed. If she needed a wee, she waited until she got back home. She had a fastidious streak. From time to time he felt her disapproval. No Jo this morning. Something must have cropped up. No Ella either. It hadn't mattered. He had woken at twelve and opened up the shop himself.

He leant backwards, hollowing his lumbar, in order to look in the bathroom glass. He saw himself – not from the inside looking down, the landscape which began with glimpses of alternate sides of his nose and went all the way down to his feet and somehow translated itself into the fellow in the mirror – but as someone quite separate. He had the sun tan from the neck up and on the lower arms from lounging outside the shop – and Lois's good head of hair. He paid attention to his clothes, choosing what he hoped was a raffish style and incorporating this and that from the house clearance to keep the cost down. But it had to be faced that his body had lost its bowling-green flatness. He had had the best part of a week to whittle away the gentle curve to his belly before he met Francesca again but he had done nothing – unless he counted his walk with Ella on Thursday evening. He had nearly forgotten that. He had gone to The Dog and was sitting in his usual spot by the corner window. She had passed by looking a bit forlorn. He had bobbed up and hailed her. She'd glared until she realised it was him. She had a sort of force field of touch-me-not and touch-paper about her which was attractive if you didn't mind risking having your head bitten off. She'd said hullo through the open window and asked him if he had a spare cigarette. He'd offered her a drink but she had said she was going for a walk. He had asked if he could accompany her. He'd said they would have to stick to the level; he couldn't manage an ascent after work. They'd both had a cigarette and set off. She'd been good company. He couldn't remember what they'd talked about. But the flavour of it he retained – cheerful and friendly, mildly flirtatious. Remembering the taste of the butterscotch but forgetting it was called Something and Something – that's how it was when your memory was going. Who gave a toss about Something and Something? They'd covered about three miles over the dunes footpaths. When he stopped for a breather she'd said they could turn back if he liked, and that made him feel like great grandad. It was the first long walk he'd had in years. Callard & Bowser. That was it. What crap he remembered.

7

'I'm not going to The Dog,' Ella said.

'Suit yourself. Where do you want to go?' Vince said.

'Round here. Not back my way,' Ella said.

'That should be interesting.' He stopped.

They had been walking slowly through the recreation ground and had reached the main road. The temperature had hardly dropped, though the sun had gone from the sky.

'Well, there's The World's Your Oyster. That's where Dad goes. Have you been there?' he said.

'No.'

'I thought not. You'd have to be seriously into sociology. Then there's The Duke of Edinburgh. Plate glass and swimming in bleach. I've never seen anyone in there, ever. In fact, it could be the mortuary. And the Sandrock Hotel. That's it.'

'Do they check up on how old you are?'

'Which one?'

'The last one. The sand something.'

'No, not as far as I know. I've never had any trouble.'

'Let's go there.'

'Don't say I didn't warn you,' Vince said.

The sole advantage of the Sandrock Hotel, and one that didn't matter to Ella and Vince, was the car park. It was the size of a small airfield. A concrete expanse without marked spaces. You could park in its furthest corners and be sure of privacy. You could park in the middle to the same effect, but the clients felt more comfortable tucked round the edges. Theft, vandalism and illicit dealing were a problem, but the landlady had a way of evading the crime prevention officer, who came round, at least once a month, with brochures full of pictures of exterior lighting. She knew what she was doing. Everyone was marooned on a separate Windsor chair, with low tables at knee level. (Ring marks etched into the dark veneer.) It was impossible, therefore, to lean on or across the table, make covert approaches under the table or cuddle up next to someone. The moment of needing to go to the car park was delayed by several hours and she sold a lot of drink.

It was funny in a cheerless way, but not that funny.

'So, what happened yesterday after you left?' asked Vince, shifting around to find the least tortured position in relation to his pint.

'Nothing. I walked along the beach. Then I went to Lois Lucas's,' said Ella. 'It wasn't eventful. Just a night.'

'Are they usually?'

'What?'

'Eventful.'

'No. Should they be?'

Vince shook his head.

'Just seemed to me you probably went out a lot,' he said.

'Not particularly,' she said.

The conversation at the next table encroached.

'I looked at my hand and it was all red and puffy with this thing on. My sister said it was a ganglion. It's disgusting isn't it? She said I should go to the doctor.'

'What did he say?'

'The receptionist thingy woman asked me to be there for eight. I couldn't believe it. Fucking liberty. You know me. I'm not a morning person, never have been.'

'Weird, the way people say that,' Ella said.

108

'Say what?' Vince said.

'Never have been,' she said. 'As if it wasn't enough just to be.'

'What are you on about?'

'You know. I am this consistent person. Cut me wherever you like and I'll still say Folkestone Rock.'

'Or Frying Tonight,' Vince said.

'It wouldn't say that.'

'No, I suppose not. It was the smell made me think of it. But you're like that.'

'What?'

'The same, through and through,' Vince said.

'No I'm not,' Ella said.

The Sandrock Hotel was filling up. The atmosphere had turned to smoke. There was no air conditioning, just a small electric fan that pointed towards the bar staff. It was standing on a beer towel to stop it walking off the edge of the counter top. People who hadn't had a cigarette for years went to the vending machine and bought a packet and were grateful. They weren't regulars, or, at least, not regulars from nearby. Couples came here from towns along the coast, confident they wouldn't meet anyone they knew. A man standing behind Vince had struck unlucky and was laughing too loudly and failing to introduce his woman. Ella seemed transfixed by them. Vince, hearing the laugh, looked over his shoulder to see what she was looking at. When he turned back she was gone.

The last time she bolted Ella had found herself on the loose shingle by the East Kent railway line. This time she was in a dingy hallway at the back of the hotel. It was quiet, cut off from the noise of the bar by the walls and the old velvet curtains that hung dustily over them. In front of her was a flight of stairs with a cardboard notice saying Private propped on the bottom step. Behind her was the door from the bar that said the same. The Sandrock Hotel had no bedrooms for guests, in spite of its name. She moved the notice to a higher step and sat down and rested her head on her knees. The carpet in the dark gap between her feet was grubby and fixed with a tarnished stair rod. Her right leg was shaking. She couldn't stop it. Panic was still rising in her like pumped water in a tank.

She tried to concentrate on the image that had ejected her. From the ordinary pattern of people and glasses and bottles and smoke, some fragment had produced an uprush of recognition. A quarter of a head of dark hair, a sliver of blue shoulder, like a piece of sky in a jigsaw puzzle, a bare elbow. A kaleidoscope trick. She didn't trust herself to know whether it had been Felpo or not. She must be unhinged, she thought – as bad as Vince's nan, only fifty years younger.

The back hallway of the Sandrock Hotel was dark and smelled of those blocks that people hooked over the rim of their toilets. Ella couldn't stay there. The smell and the notice marked Private unnerved her. Whoever lived in the place was entitled to do whatever they wanted beyond that point. They might finish what they were doing and come down the stairs. She listened for scuffling or talking but upstairs was silent. She only heard the faint thud of music coming from the bar.

There was another door to the side of the stairs. It was barricaded by a table, with a leafless potted plant on it. She got up from the step, lifted the plant, light with dryness, on to the floor and moved the table away. The door had bolts that had been painted in, but she managed to move them. Flakes of toughened paint fell on to the carpet. She wondered what was on the other side and hesitated for a few moments. She had lost her sense of direction and didn't want to walk in on some sideline business of the landlady. But when she opened the door cautiously the night air that came through the gap was real. She was out in the car park.

'What happened to you?' asked Vince, when he found her. 'I've been looking for you for the last half hour. I hung around the front. I walked up to the main road. I went in the Ladies. I even went in the Gents. I came round the back here. I was just bracing myself to start looking in the cars. What are you doing sitting on the ground, anyway?'

'I felt sick,' said Ella.

'You must have moved fast. Levitation or something.'

He was standing over her and she could see him shifting from foot to foot in front of her. She didn't reply.

'I saw some woman do that at the Odeon in Dover when I was a kid,' he said. 'I refused to go again for about a year and then it closed down.'

A car on the far side of the car park, as dormant as the others, suddenly started into life. The headlights went on, windows were lowered, gristly singing burst out and was instantly consumed by an overused accelerator. The car sped past, bucking at the bumps at the exit, like a boy doing stunts on a bike.

'What was the film?' asked Ella, raising her head.

'I can't remember,' said Vince.

'But you remember the levitation bit.'

'That wasn't in the film. It was real. She was sitting in the row in front.' He looked down at her. 'Are you going to stay there all night? Because I'm going home.'

'No, I'll come too. Vince, can you do me a favour?'

She leant forward and rubbed her shin. It had stopped shaking, but still felt peculiar.

'I thought I might walk past my house and see if anyone's there. If they're not, I'll go and sleep there,' she said.

'I told you to do that right from the start,' he said.

He paused. She still hadn't got up. 'Well, what's the favour?'

'Could you come with me?' she said.

A couple came out of the hotel and walked past them to their car. The woman, who was only wearing one shoe, was clutching a handful of the man's shirt and trying to keep upright.

Vince was looking puzzled.

'You mean, I walk all the way over to your place, drop you off and walk all the way back,' he said.

'Yes,' said Ella.

'All right,' said Vince. 'But I wish you'd thought of it before, then we could have gone to The Dog.'

'I'm sorry,' said Ella.

'You've never said that before,' he said. 'Ever.'

She looked over his shoulder at the far side of the car park.

'Let's get moving, then. It's going to take a while to get over there,' he said.

He pulled her to her feet and kept hold of her hands, but once she stood up she shrugged him off.

8

They were all startled by the doorbell. The television was on and no one had spoken for nearly an hour.

'I'll go,' Rob said.

He got up from the sofa.

'Who is it?' Dilys said.

'I'll come with you, son,' Geoff said. 'It's late.'

'If it's that duster boy,' Dilys said, 'put the chain on.'

Jo listened, suddenly brought back to her present surroundings. She had been in the mental equivalent of half-light; groping around, bumping against her thoughts. The intent look on Rob's face made her more alert. She heard the door open – opened wide without the check of the chain – then a man's voice, then Geoff's.

'Who is it?' Dilys said.

'I don't know, Gran,' Jo said.

Rob came back into the room and collapsed back on the sofa. He curled both hands over his nose as he used to do when he sucked his thumb.

'He doesn't say who it is,' Dilys said. 'Can't have been anyone.'

For a moment Jo had hoped – a freakish lift to her spirits. But the hope had been stupid.

They heard the front door shut. Geoff returned to the sitting room.

'That was Gareth, Marion's boy. He's asked us in for a tipple,' he said.

'Whatever for?' Dilys said.

'He said he wanted to say thank you to us for looking after Marion when she had the burglars.'

'Very nice of him,' Dilys said.

'I said we'd just look in. We won't have to stay long,' he said.

Dilys looked at him in astonishment.

'Why not?' Geoff said. 'We're just staring at the four walls. It'll be nice for Jo to get out.'

'She won't want to go anywhere,' Dilys said.

'She might,' Geoff said.

'Oh, come on, Gran,' Jo said. 'Let's just go.'

She pulled herself out of the armchair before she changed her mind.

'No, I'd have to put my other shoes on,' Dilys said. 'I'll stay with Annie.'

'I'm not moving,' Rob said.

Marion had a soft thick carpet the colour of porridge and a well stocked drinks cabinet with a little light inside. There were several comfortable chairs squashed close together and a large coffee table bearing bowls of crisps and nuts and olives with red centres. The lighting was low, coming from shaded wall fittings. Two matching vases of pink, shop-bought chrysanthemums balanced on the mantelpiece. The effect was luxurious compared with their house next door. Jo felt, as she walked in, that she was looking at a framed picture on the far side of a room, somewhere self-contained and separate from the turmoil in her mind. She hadn't been out to anyone's house for months. She wasn't sure she knew what to do.

She sat down and Gareth poured the drinks. He said he'd spent the afternoon trying to scrub the glass-fitter's putty marks off the window. It had been some sort of indestructible putty, more like chewing gum. Marion, with the brave bright lipstick shakily applied to her powdery lips, retold the story of the burglary. Jo paid attention to the relevant features: the drawers of the lacquered desk that the burglar had opened, the replacement pane of glass which Gareth had cleaned up that afternoon. No one interrupted, although they all knew the sequence of events. Gareth topped up the drinks then sat next to her, his legs stretched out, looking too big for the room.

Jo began to relax, finding it restful to be with these people who didn't know her but were well disposed towards her. Dilys and Geoff had put in the graft by being neighbourly over the years, and because she was their granddaughter she was given alcohol and plied with salty nibbles. When Marion asked her what her news was, she found, with the help of the sparkling wine, that she was able to answer. She said that Annie was due to start at nursery school in September and that Rob had been on a life-saving course at the local swimming baths during the holidays. Ella would be taking GCSEs next summer. She said what amazing weather they had had for the last couple of months and how not going away didn't matter when the kids could be out of doors. All that sort of thing. It sounded, to her ears, not entirely plausible. As she mentioned each of her children she could see them peacefully conforming – looking as if they lived with a different mother and smelled of newly ironed clothes. Marion smiled and nodded, not disappointed in the slightest by the meagre information. Gareth was jocular and chipped in with similar facts about his own pair who were university age. They would both need driving to their respective destinations for the beginning of the new term: Falmouth and Ripon. They could hardly be further apart so they'd use two cars. Paula would take the route west because she didn't like the M1 and he'd do Yorkshire. We could go on like this for hours, Jo thought, and what we said wouldn't be true or untrue.

The wine made her sleepy. There was no need to say anything significant, or make particular sense. Marion posed the well-meaning questions about her plans for the rest of the week and the cut on her face. She dealt with them as if they were someone else's intentions or memories, saying more or less what she had said to Dilys about not having decided – and the gas stove. Then they talked about gardening in the drought. Then it was time to leave.

'Marion's a good sort,' Geoff said as they went back up the front path. 'Perked you up to have a change of scene. I was worried about you.'

'We haven't been out together for a long time, have we?' Jo said.

Geoff shook his head and smiled, remembering those occasions when they had eluded Dilys and got away to the local pub for a pint in the late afternoon. She and Geoff had been the only ones in the bar who talked. The others, a handful of solitary men, including the barman, read the paper and smoked, grunted to one another on arriving and leaving.

As if recalling the quiet of that far-away time, they stood for a while in the front garden listening to the street noises. They could hear the hum of the traffic on the main road and rowdy male shouts. Someone in a house further down was practising drumming – a ripple of thuds followed by fitful banging.

9

It was quiet off the main routes from the Channel ports. From time to time cars leaving the Sandrock Hotel swept past them, riding the bends. Sheep munched in the nearby fields. The dark had settled on them but they carried on eating. Ella and Vince went single file. They didn't talk. They reached the outer edges of the town and the small housing developments that were set away from the road. They were safer off the fast road but the town didn't feel quite safe. It wasn't, but unless they were unlucky the trouble would happen somewhere else: asylum seekers and local thugs slugging it out, asylum seekers and rival asylum seekers slugging it out, drug dealing tipping into violence. Most of the rest was predictable, the kind of stuff that's been going on for centuries: drunkenness, smuggling, domestic commotion, domestic brutality. Some of it might have spilled on to the street, though not on that particular night. The rest was out of sight.

The road suddenly narrowed. Clapboard houses crowded together. The old town had a few hours to be itself, to close out the present and go back in time, though the light wasn't right. There shouldn't have been light at all, except from the sky. Some of the windows made squares of brightish haze behind drawn curtains. People were hidden inside — insomniacs who had given up the pretence of sleep, the sick and the anxious dozing in front of videos, wakeful babies.

The street lamps stayed on but there were dense patches of darkness between the houses and around the old churches.

They reached Ella's house about an hour after leaving the Sandrock Hotel. The ground-floor flat was hidden by drawn blinds. Upstairs a light was on and both front windows were open, top and bottom. Ella looked for a van – battered and covered in swirls of colour – but it had gone. She and Vince stood staring up. They could see the back of one of the green-painted chairs up against the kitchen window – just the struts with spaces in between. There was no one sitting on it. She saw the pots and pans on the shelf above the stove and the edge of the calendar that her gran had sent at Christmas. She couldn't remember the August picture. The squares for the days were mostly blank because her mother only wrote down things like the dentist – not what actually happened. Ella wanted to return to Friday morning, living inside the minutes when she watched her mother washing Annie's hands at the sink, locking herself away till the danger was past. But she had missed the chance to leave life as it was. She hadn't understood then that this was an option that could be consciously taken.

She nudged Vince.

'Let's go,' she said.

They turned round and didn't speak again until they were further down the road. The Dog had turned out an hour or so ago. It was shut-up and peaceful. No one was about.

'Shame those people downstairs weren't in,' Vince said.

'I don't really know them,' Ella said.

'We had Christians next door once. They put a leaflet through the door called *Controlling Children through the Power of Prayer*,' Vince said.

'Your mum wouldn't have liked that,' Ella said.

'She went ape.'

They carried on walking.

'I think he was in there,' Vince said.

'Who?'

'Your mum's boyfriend.'

'Probably,' she said.

'Are you scared of him?'

'No,' she said.

They stopped outside Lois Lucas & Son. The building looked featureless out of hours, part of the street. A boy passed by on the other side, kicking a tin can on and off the kerb. The hollow din sounded in the silence. The boy was too alone and cowardly to find his voice and yell abuse. Vince peered through the glass of the shop.

'Not a lot going on, is there?' He kept his voice low.

'No,' said Ella. She got out her key. 'You go.'

'Are you really spending the night here?'

'Yes,' she said.

'I'll wait till you're inside,' Vince said.

'No,' she said. 'It would feel weird, with you looking in. Like being a dummy in a shop window. I wouldn't like it.'

'Do you think Trevor's there?'

'I've no idea. I wish you'd shut up about him.'

Vince moved away from the window.

'You're all right now? You're not feeling sick any more?' he said.

'I'm fine. Promise. You go,' she said.

She gave him a small shove in the back. He set off down the street. At the corner he stopped and turned round. Ella was still standing outside the shop. He hesitated. She waved. He looked away again and broke into a run. She waited until his footsteps died away – and unlocked the door.

Ella felt restless. She took off her shoes and padded over the floorboards. She picked things up and put them down again. She arranged the jugs and vases in order of height on a sideboard. One of them had a dead fly at the bottom. It had dropped, dopey, in mid-flight and starved. A sudden lurching fall. Then, looking round for something else to occupy her, she decided to put all the figurines together on a dresser shelf. She gathered them up – any tat with a head or a face – and placed them in pairs so that they seemed as if they might be talking to each other. The balloon lady with the Home Pride flour man, a glass mouse with St Francis. Her scene needed a background, a street scene or a garden. She found a place mat of Windsor Castle and propped it up behind the figures. She heard a creak above, somewhere over her head. The building made noises. Because it was old it adjusted, shifted position. She was nervous of the noises, so, in order not to set them off, she walked more carefully. She went across to the place where she'd slept the night before. Opposite her was a full-length mirror, propped at an angle. She felt uneasy about having slept in view of it as if it might have acted like a video camera recording her. She caught sight of herself across the two lengths of floor, the real floor and the one beyond the mirror that sloped downwards. She put her tongue out, but she couldn't, at this distance, see the girl in the reflection doing the same. The girl was pale and young-looking. She started to lay out her bed – the cushion and the blanket of knitted squares. Without even looking in the mirror she saw herself repeating the actions of the previous night: unfolding the blanket, spreading it out, plumping up the cushion. Playing. 'You'll stay there forever, will you, gathering dust?' Vince had asked her and she'd thought it a stupid thing to say, because, of course, she wasn't going to stay forever.

She hadn't made any plans. She had kept her thoughts at bay – though she sensed them there waiting to rush in. If her mum's face got better . . . If Felpo stayed away. These were the good thoughts. She felt that her life, as she had known it, was over. She hoped, maybe, one day, she could have a parallel but lesser existence, eating, sleeping, working, maybe even getting a shadowy boyfriend and having shadowy children – passing the time until she was an old lady. The shadowiness wouldn't be visible from the outside, but she wouldn't pretend to be the self she used to be. She sat down on the blanket with her back supported by the staircase and rested her head on her knees.

The telephone was ringing. Ella started. She must have dozed off. Then she was confused, thinking it might be morning. On and on it rang, rattling the china standing next to it – old-style loudness that matched its bulky shape – separate and demanding, with a life of its own. The room was still dark – it wasn't morning – but she didn't know how much time had passed. She thought she heard movement upstairs, feet on the floor. Maybe the door clicked open. She tucked herself into a neater shape. With any luck she would be out of sight. The angle that the mirror was leaning at wasn't steep enough to throw her reflection up. She waited for Trevor's irregular pattern of steps, his hand steady on the handrail. He had a boozer's respect for stairs. That wasn't a good way to go, he said. She felt suddenly responsible for him. What would she do if he tripped and fell all the way down? Seeing her might be enough of a shock to give him a heart attack. She had forgotten what the recovery position was. They'd shown them a video on first aid at school but she hadn't paid attention. He would go grey and make sick gurgling noises. She knew how he'd look – though not how to help.

Ella hugged her knees tighter. The ringing continued. Trevor still didn't come down. She was puzzled – then afraid.

The telephone stopped and the reverberations with it. Her ears didn't adjust straight away. The silence was a sheer drop. She leapt up and threw herself towards the door, knocking into things as she went.

10

Trevor was on his way back from Borrowdale. He wasn't a tidy walker, but he built up a weary momentum and this took him along. The street was wide and repeated itself. Similar houses were set back behind the remains of Edwardian shrubberies, separated by scatterings of dead leaves from the evergreens' summer shedding. There were differences in detail, but the darkness suppressed them. He had left the car at home. He used to drive everywhere, however much he'd drunk, until he found himself late one night on a surface which didn't feel like the road and the only sure way of finding out was by opening the car door and sticking out his foot. He had guessed he was on some soft sandy part of the Sandwich Golf Course and confirmed this when his vision had partially returned and he'd seen a little flag on a stick. The episode had shaken him. He had been more careful after that. Death wasn't too bad, but you couldn't depend on outright death. Near misses didn't bear thinking about.

He had spent the end of the evening with Francesca. He'd turned up at Borrowdale at around ten. Lights out for the oldsters. He had tapped on the door. There was a doorbell set in a large marble surround. For Admittance to the Home after 5 p.m. Please Ring the Bell. Thank you. But he hadn't liked to press it. Francesca had let him in after a few minutes. She hadn't looked surprised to see him. She had already taken off the overall – it was the first time he'd seen her without it – and was wearing a lace vest and a skirt made of some thin black material. She hadn't wasted time. They'd shared the bottle of wine he'd brought with him and talked about the mundane things they had done during the week. She hadn't flirted with him but everything had flowed in the same direction. It had been a funny place for love. A room off the front office with a desk and a couch where Matron talked to relatives. Not conducive in sheer aesthetic terms but he'd felt more rejuvenated than he had done for a while. They'd ignored the whimpers and the moans, the cries for Nurse. He'd been coasting home, feeling fairly complacent. Then, at the first loud thump and incoherent shout from down the passage, she'd turned dutiful. She'd moved fast, up and, with a bit of rearrangement, out of the door. It was all right for women. No one had done that to him since he was seventeen. Well, eighteen. In a borrowed car up on the Downs.

As he turned the corner onto the home stretch he fumbled in his trouser pocket for his keys. Something about the street struck him as odd for the time of night. He couldn't quite put his finger on it but it looked more lived-in somehow, cosier, like an evening in winter. When he got close enough he saw why that was. Light from the window of Lois Lucas & Son was illuminating the pavement in front of it, extending into the road. The empty milk bottles glinted. Cheerful as the run-up to Christmas. He knew he hadn't left a light on. The sun had still been shining when he left. Kids, he thought, and wondered if they were still in there. Bloody pests. The night wasn't going to be palliated by oblivion; the essential rest from today's and tomorrow's blundering. Old age reached out to him; the sameness of days, the binding limitations. He wouldn't say no to it if it were offered to him. But he hadn't quite got there. He rubbed a hand across his forehead and then down over his face, pulling it out of shape. He was outside the shop now. He stared through the glass. A lighted lamp was lying on the floor, otherwise it was the usual shambles. The door was flaky but intact. He unlocked it and pushed. Then, just in case, he held it open, as if he were a bored commissionaire, and waited.

After a few seconds he went inside and nothing else seemed amiss. The shop still held the day's heat. He stood the lamp upright again. The bulb flickered and then came on brightly. Perhaps a cat had got in through the kitchen window. He wandered into the lean-to. The mugs were lined up on the windowsill. They all had some horrible liquid in them, at different levels of fullness. He piled them into the sink and turned on the tap. Only cold water at this hour of the night. The hot water came on at ten. He decided against coffee and went back into the shop.

'Tired am I,' he said aloud.

Lois used to say that. Proclaim it. He never got the intonation right. He could see her now holding on to the newel post at the bottom of the stairs, preparing for the ascent. At the end she couldn't make it. Her breathing was too bad and her legs wouldn't go. He couldn't carry her up. Her body was too solid – compact she called it. He shut the shop and made a bed up for her downstairs, nice and clean with all the trimmings. Half a dozen white pillows and the satin eiderdown. She couldn't settle though. She only put up with the arrangement for a week. She lay there pricing everything up and fretted without the customers. The regulars pushed cards and little gifts that would fit through the letter-box. Soap and cassette tapes and miniature bottles of whisky. She didn't want visitors – not there, nor at the cottage hospital where she spent the last month. Someone sent a book of poems and prayers – *A Celtic Miscellany*. He remembered her wheezing with laughter. Finally she got it out. She thinks I'm Welsh, she said. Welsh. He was perplexed. Not necessarily, Mother, he said. Oh yes she does, she does, she said and carried on heaving and trying to get her breath.

He was preparing to climb the stairs himself, taking one last look round. There was a clearing amongst the clutter. He suddenly noticed it. He stood and stared, transfixed by the knitted blanket laid out in a neat rectangle with a cushion at its head. His first thought was that Lois never could have got down on the floor. He closed his eyes and opened them again. So someone *had* been in the shop.

There was something innocent about the arrangement – not the style of a tramp. Tramps didn't play house. And whoever came in had a key. Ella then. There was no one else it could have been. He wondered whether to give Jo a call, but it was too late, or too early. He hadn't seen either of them for a day or two. He felt apprehensive, but casting his mind back, he couldn't retrieve anything significant. Jo had seemed fine, and Ella too. He had lost track of time. He'd been for that walk with her. She hadn't looked like someone who was in trouble or about to run away. She'd been disgruntled at first but she had soon cheered up. He could be mistaken, but he put his money on their both being happy at that point – mother and daughter. He wasn't one of those types who think everything is a sham. People led lives right up to the second when everything went haywire. Oblivious they were to what life was about to chuck at them.

He bent down and picked up the bedding. He hung the blanket over a wooden towel rail and lobbed the cushion at the top of the wardrobe. A pallet for one it had been. Whatever reason Ella had for making her bed there it wasn't fornication. She was below the age of consent, of course – though that never stopped them. He was thinking more that a girl like her would prefer to be on the beach out in the open – or on the side of a bed that was nearer the door. After dark, she'd need the reassurance of a running figure in lights who resembled herself – and the Exit sign. She wouldn't let herself get trapped indoors with a fellow.

He walked over to the window, cupped his hands round his face and pressed it to the glass. No sign of life, but there was a trace of light in the sky. The day had keeled over into the next. Sunday, he thought. They'll be round with the papers, and ringing the bell for whatever they call it – Holy Communion – in a few hours. Francesca would go off duty, yawning and waiting for the day staff to show up. He needed to sleep but he felt too lazy to go upstairs. He stretched himself out on one of the tip-up theatre seats. Companionable it was down here. Like a dormitory. Lois and Ella and God knew who else. All of them – dead or alive – who had ever had forty winks in this room.

11

Ella ran through the town and didn't stop running until she could taste open air. She walked back to the main Dover road. She was always walking. Sometimes she covered distance without noticing her surroundings, surprised to arrive at whichever place she regained consciousness, her body powered by strange energy. At other times, and going at a similar speed, she was aware of the nearby landscape going by so slowly, sticking to her, rising and falling minutely with each sequence of steps. The fields beside the wide road stretched away on either side, as domestic as large gardens in the night. The road passed through them. Only the sky was a comfort – not a place where she was known.

She reached the fast road. Although it was around three in the morning there was still some traffic – cars and container lorries that rattled past. She kept close to the side.

A car slowed down and pulled in about twenty metres ahead of her. She approached the red tail-lights intending to walk past. She heard the doors' central locking click open. The driver turned his head but he didn't lean over. The window was electric and had already slid down.

'Where are you heading for?' he said.

His voice was matter of fact and he didn't smile. If he'd leant over or smiled she would have run away. She guessed he was about forty. Not young, anyway.

'I'm going to France,' he said. 'Catching the first ferry of the day from Dover.'

'All right,' she said. 'Dover's fine.'

She watched him lean across and move a pile of documents from the passenger seat to the back. He didn't switch the engine off. It was still ticking over. He opened the door and she got in. He indicated before he pulled away, and checked his mirror, though there were no other cars on the road. Their seats were quite far apart with a wide carpety island between them. The car smelled of clothes that have come back from the dry cleaners. Cleanish, but mixed up with other people's lives. Out of the corner of her right eye she could see a white shirt with a jacket over it, hanging behind the driving seat.

'Better put your seat belt on,' he said.

They were moving already and gaining speed. She couldn't change her mind. Direction signs appeared ahead. Signs on stilts that were easy to read as you rushed towards them, but which she would have had to walk underneath, had she still been walking. She fastened the belt. He wasn't talkative and he didn't play music. But eventually he spoke.

'I'm going to a wedding way down in the middle of France. Friend of mine is marrying a girl from St Etienne. Her first marriage, his second. The triumph of hope over experience. It's a hell of a drive. But why not?'

Ella was shocked to be spoken to and surprised by the pattern his voice made. She had nothing to say. She had never heard of the place he'd mentioned.

'You've probably been a bridesmaid?' he said.

'No.'

'Shame. You'd enjoy it. A chance to dress up in frilly clothes instead of the regulation jeans and T-shirt. Bit of make-up and you'd be away. If you take a look behind you, you'll see the present. On the back seat.'

Ella stared at the dashboard that glimmered with luminous green data and wondered what the time was.

'Go on. Have a look,' he said.

She turned and glanced briefly at a chunky gold parcel

topped with a matching rosette. It looked like one of the fake Christmas gifts they put under the tree in the local garage.

'Guess what it is?'

She shook her head.

'Three guesses. Go on.'

She said nothing.

'I'll give you a clue. It weighs a ton.'

She tried now, because she wanted him to be quiet, but she couldn't think of a single object that would fit in a box that size – or any size. Heavy or light. It was as if she existed in a universe with nothing in it.

'Think kitchen.'

She was silent.

'Cookery programmes on the TV. Go on. What have those grinning idiots always got?'

She shook her head and wound the bottom of her T-shirt into a ball.

'I'll shut up,' he said.

They drove on.

'There's a roundabout coming up. It would be no trouble for me to go round it and back the way we came,' the man said. 'I'd take you home.'

'No, it's all right,' Ella said.

'Where was it in Dover you wanted to go?' he said. 'I'm going to the ferry terminal but I'll drop you wherever you like.'

She wiped her nose with the back of her hand.

'There will be fine,' she said.

'Where?'

'Where you said. The ferry terminal.'

'We turn off soon,' he said. 'To the Eastern Docks. Sure that's what you want?'

She nodded. She had no idea where she was going. She thought she might leave England though she couldn't see beyond the journey. She had gone with her French class on a day trip to Calais. The cross-Channel ferry had been a world of its own, like a fun fair with bars and shops. Apart from the safety regulations there weren't any rules. Everyone seemed to do as they pleased and when they got bored with one part of the boat they moved on to another. Even in an hour and a half she had come to recognise the same people. She had passed them on the stairs.

'You don't have much luggage,' the man said.

'My mum's got it,' she said.

'Where is she?'

'With my gran and grandad.'

'How about your dad?'

'He's in Dover already.'

The man nodded, as if working things out. Perhaps he had enough to go on to make a kind of story. A holiday where everyone made their own travel arrangements and somehow met up – like the stable at Bethlehem. You didn't have to tell people much for them to go off following some trail.

'I've got a daughter, I mentioned her, didn't I?' he said. 'A bit younger than you. How old are you?'

Ella hesitated.

'You don't have to tell me,' he said.

The roundabout was at the bottom of the hill. He drove round it and stopped at the traffic lights on one of the exit roads.

'We're nearly there,' he said. 'I've got a suggestion. I drive on to the dock and park up. Then we call your mum or dad on my mobile and tell them you're safe. There's a café there. We can have a cup of something while we're waiting.'

'No,' she said.

'No to which bit?' he said.

'Just drop me,' she said. 'I'll be fine.'

'Where?' he said.

'At that café. The one you said. We're all meeting up there.' She glanced at the clock. She still couldn't make it out. 'At five o'clock. I'm a bit early. But they'll turn up. They're really reliable.'

'I thought you said your dad would be waiting for you.'

'He is. The others I meant.'

He nodded but she could tell that he was doubtful. Her idea of mingling with the crowd on the ferry, making new friends, evaporated under his questioning. He wasn't even asking her anything personal.

'I'm not supposed to take lifts,' she said. 'It's best if my dad doesn't find out.'

He winked at her.

They drove on to the dock. An expanse of tarmac lay ahead, divided by painted lines that were nearly invisible in the darkness. At the far end were cars standing in rows and, beyond, the pale bulk of a boat. The café was to one side – isolated and no more than a brightly lit shack. Ella undid her seat belt.

'Drop me here, please,' she said. 'I'll walk across.'

'No,' her companion said. 'I'll see you right.'

He swerved in a half circle and stopped abruptly by the café with a screech of brakes.

'Thanks for the lift,' she said.

He nodded and started to scrabble round in the glove compartment.

She opened the car door and got out.

'Bye,' she said, into the night air.

She didn't turn round again. She hoped he would drive away and join one of the queues but the car wasn't moving. She only had a few steps to go to the café. In that time she heard the engine switch off. She walked straight through the open door of the café.

'El.'

She knew whose voice it was. She glanced round. Cans of Fanta were stacked in a pyramid on the counter and behind them a woman with her hair tied up in a scarf was reading a magazine. Beige-coloured water trickled from the tea and coffee dispenser. There was only one customer. He had an empty plastic cup and an empty bottle of beer in front of him. The table he was sitting at was red with a chipped metal edge. Ella couldn't leave the café. The man in the car was waiting for her. She and Felpo looked at one another. She saw surprise in his eyes but it didn't spread to the rest of his face.

'Where's Jo?' Felpo said after a few moments. The question was without urgency, as if he'd come back from work and wondered which room Jo was in. He bent slightly, as if trying to see out of the window.

'She's in London,' Ella said.

She sat down opposite him.

'Oh,' Felpo said. 'I thought for a moment she was with you. Stupid. She wasn't at home when I went back. I kept putting it off – going back. I cleared up and packed my stuff in the van.' He hesitated. 'But you say she's in London.'

'Yes,' said Ella. 'She went with Rob and Annie.'

'Did she say how long she'd be there?' he said.

'No.'

'Did she say anything?'

Ella was silent. Felpo was far off in thought and gazing past her.

'You weren't in the shop then?' she said.

'When?'

'Tonight.'

He shook his head and seemed puzzled.

'What would I go there for?' he said.

'I don't know,' she said.

'What are you doing here anyway?' Felpo said. 'At this time of night.' He spoke the last sentence as if it were the punch line of a joke but she wasn't annoyed.

'I didn't want to go with them,' she said.

'But why here?' he said.

'Something to do,' she said.

He smiled but he didn't comment. He never fussed about their safety.

Ella looked at him. He had had that same expression when he came to the shop for the first time – blank but sort of exposed. He seemed to read her mind.

'You never liked me, did you?' he said. 'I kept hoping you'd change your mind.'

She recoiled inside and shifted her eyes away. She didn't want to have to think about whether she liked him or not.

'It's all right,' he said. 'You don't have to answer.'

She could sense his stillness and it unsettled her. It was always there, underneath his liveliness. It never went away. She concentrated on what he'd just said – what he had actually said – isolated from her reaction. She examined it and found it neutral, like the expression on his face. She'd hated him but she had exaggerated. Her thoughts about him had got out and stuck to him, layer on layer. That used to happen to unlucky kids at school, who attracted rejection because of some puny difference: the wrong kind of coat, freckly hands. Once the rejection had got a hold it was added to and added to, until the person inside was invisible, a thing.

'What did you say to me on Friday morning?' she asked suddenly.

'I thought you did most of the talking,' he said.

'About seeing me with Trevor,' she said.

'That was it, wasn't it?' he said.

'You said,' Ella stopped. She remembered, but she couldn't say the words out loud. It was embarrassing to be able to repeat exactly what he said to her. Talk should fly away. She couldn't stand people who stored up things you said and handed them back to you.

'Go on,' he said.

She was silent. When she thought what boys said to her on the street, what they shouted out of car windows. She never cared. They could say what they liked.

She had met him on her way to the beach. He'd parked his van and was heading down to the boats. She hadn't wanted to talk to him, but she hadn't been able to avoid him. He asked her if she'd had a good evening. Nice down on the dunes, he said. He kept pace with her. They were going in the same direction. She started to cross the road but a car came past and he caught her elbow and pulled her back. She immediately straightened her arm so that his hand was left suspended. She asked him what he was on about. You were with Trevor. I thought it was you, anyway, he said. He's a bit of a mystery man, isn't he? The words had enraged her. What were you doing down there, she said. He told her he had been in the van, on the road before the low bridge. I pulled in, he said. *Pulled in*. She had fitted him into the picture then, sitting in the van, leaning back, very still, watching her, making up stupid stories about her. She wished a car had come over the bridge too fast and hit him or that a tree had fallen on top of him. You're weird, she said. He smiled, as if he had some secret information. Don't worry, he said. I wasn't that close. Really.

'I probably did say something annoying. I often do. I don't know when to stop,' he said.

She looked down at the table, at the biscuit crumbs lodged in the crack where the metal edge had come away.

'Who's that?' Felpo said suddenly, in a different voice.

'Who?'

'That bloke out there. He's looking at us.'

Ella turned round. The man who'd given her the lift was peering in. He gave a kind of wave and raised both eyebrows.

'Do you know him?' Felpo said.

'No. He was hanging around outside when I came in,' she said.

'Shall I tell him to piss off?' he said.

'No. He'll go away now he's seen you.'

Felpo stood up and made a face.

'He has done too,' he said. 'He's getting into his car. I must be scarier than I thought.' He laughed.

She heard the car drive away. The tannoy system began to crackle, then came to life with a voice that advised passengers to rejoin their vehicles.

'That's me, then. They're starting to load,' Felpo said. 'Will you be all right, El?'

She nodded.

Felpo stood up.

'Wait,' Ella said. 'I need to tell you something.'

'Well?' he said.

He didn't sound interested. He picked up the empty bottle and threw it so that it landed in the bin. Then he picked up the cup.

She and Felpo had been standing on the pavement in the sunshine. She remembered the adverts for price cuts in the window of the Co-op and the hanging baskets of red busy Lizzies waving from the house with the green trellis. A man had gone by on a bike. Everything had suddenly been in the sharpest of colours – clearer than life. She had said, Jo and Trevor were probably looking for a quiet place to have a shag. The words had come ready-made in her mouth as if someone else had put them there – quick as a sneeze – and yet they bore the imprint of her personality. They were her. They were as familiar as the shape of her hands. She couldn't disown them.

She said he didn't see anything did he? He made all this stuff up and he didn't see what was really going on. She said Jo was always shutting the shop for a couple of hours: the blind down and the closed sign up. She and Trevor liked doing it with people walking by outside. It was like being on stage with the curtains down. He wasn't to think that his turning up was going to stop it. Not for more than five minutes. He was a kind of blip. Jo was probably trying to

135

make Trevor jealous. Whatever it was, it had worked. It was on again. He would soon notice that they were seeing each other every day and calling each other. They would go out in the middle of the night, like last time. Driving to some parking place. They weren't particularly careful. None of them would mind. Not even Annie. Where did he think *she* came from when her parents weren't getting on? Why did he think Trevor was so nice to her? The story was out of control – full of holes and the holes growing bigger. She had left Felpo and started to run. People had stared at her. She'd got to the sea and then she hadn't known where to go. She was sure he'd tell Jo. There would be a row. She'd have to style it out. She had run back towards home. She had stepped out in front of a lorry. The driver had shouted at her. She'd knocked into an old man. She'd reached the house. She'd run up the stairs. Her mother was there, but it was different from what she'd expected.

Ella realised that she still hadn't spoken.

'It wasn't true what I said about Mum and Trevor. It was me you saw, not her,' she said.

Felpo paused fractionally – and threw the cup. That went in the bin too.

'Thanks for telling me,' he said.

She couldn't read anything in his face.

'None of it was true,' she said.

He still didn't speak.

'Doesn't it make any difference?' she said.

'Not really,' he said.

He sat down again. She waited. Cars were starting their engines.

'The lie doesn't matter. It's the least important thing about it,' he said.

'But, if I hadn't,' Ella said.

'Forget it. It was made-up. The rest was real.' He

hesitated. 'She wouldn't want me after that. I'm sorry, I can't talk about it.'

She looked down at her hands; her dirty fingernails, the silly elastic bracelets.

'You're tired,' he said. 'Why don't you go home?'

'I suppose I might,' she said.

'There's no point hanging around here,' he said.

He stood up again.

'Come on,' he said. 'I'll take you back.'

Ella stood up too but she didn't move. She jammed her hands into the back pockets of her jeans, as if she were afraid to let them out.

'Why not?' he said.

Ella dropped her head and her hair hid her face.

'I understand,' he said. He gave a sort of laugh. 'You're not taking any chances. I don't blame you. Here, call your dad and ask for a lift. Then I'll push off.'

He handed her his phone. Ella took it but hesitated, staring at it as if she were trying to read a message in a cryptic code. They told you not to lie but they never told you why. They didn't say it changed things, that it was some sort of cosmic interference.

'Do it, El,' he said. 'I've got to leave.'

She punched in the numbers. Her dad answered, muddled with sleep. She told him where she was, then cut him off. Felpo took the phone and put it back in the frayed bag he always carried around with him. He felt around in the bottom of it.

'These are yours,' he said. He pulled out his door keys. 'Take them.'

Then he left.

Sunday and Monday

1

Dilys woke her, leaning over in her night-dress. Jo hadn't heard the telephone. She got up from the sofa immediately and went through the open door to the hall, Dilys hovering behind her. She picked up the receiver that lay passive on its side next to the telephone. It had the look of an object she would remember if things turned out badly.

She turned away from Dilys and her expression of worry. She looked at the elongated shapes of red and green and yellow that the coloured panes of the front door had formed on the wall. She listened and, from time to time, cleared her throat to show Peter she was still there. His voice continued. He was very thorough in his account and in his criticism of her. She said yes and no a couple of times, and then all right, and goodbye.

Jo told Dilys as little as she could get away with about the call. Nothing about Ella accepting a lift from a stranger. Nothing about Peter and Tara going to pick her up from the ferry terminal. She couldn't face the present, so she couldn't describe it. She told her grandmother she should go back to bed. They were both standing at the bottom of the stairs.

'Please,' Jo said. 'Everything's fine. Peter's coming to pick us up. He won't be here for hours yet. We don't want to wake the children. Let's get some more rest.'

Dilys went up without speaking, looking old in her night-clothes, laid bare by the absence of beads and a collar, displaced by the early waking.

Jo returned to the front room, shutting the door on the morning light that filled the hallway and the murmur of voices from her grandparents' room upstairs. She knew what they would be saying to each other and thought of her mother, Gail, also listening to those voices, the troubled intonation, not of criticism but of fear for the future. And she felt protective towards them because they'd spent half their lives coping.

Peter must have been in a deep sleep when the telephone rang at four in the morning. He would have thought it was a wrong number. He would have asked Ella to repeat her name. When Peter said they were going out to collect Ella, Tara would have got up and put back all the make-up that she had taken off before bed. She would have made herself impeccable. Her eyes would have been spiky with mascara and excitement. She would have dressed carefully as if she were off on a business trip with a colleague she liked the look of. She and Peter would have driven in to Dover and out to the Eastern Dock. On the way Tara would have talked about maniacs, perverts, rapists, antique dealers, drug dealers, emergency vehicles, emergency contraception, alarm bells ringing in her head, which hadn't, she really couldn't understand why, rung in anybody else's.

Tara and Peter knew now about the cut on her face, Ella's leap from the train, her failure to contact Ella. She didn't blame Ella for telling them.

Although she hadn't been to chapel or church for decades, Dilys's Sundays were corseted. Jo couldn't list the precise constraints, but she could always feel them. In particular, there were a couple of hours on Sunday mornings to which different rules applied and which accounted for them, at that moment, sitting in the front room and not in the kitchen. Jo had been surprised to discover that Sundays need not be like this, that they didn't possess an essential property, like the redness of cochineal. Though, as she had grown up, she had come to see that other people's families built in different tyrannies and that the British Sunday was often part of the trap.

Filling the time could be difficult, but today they had a purpose. They were waiting not for God's grace, which hadn't been outpoured on their family for more than a generation, but for Peter to find his way there from the M2. He hadn't visited for several years and the road lay-out had changed.

'He won't know where he is,' said Geoff. 'The pubs have all got new names. Ridiculous names.'

'Don't worry, Grandad. He's used to finding his way about,' Jo said.

'They shouldn't have allowed it,' he said. 'All those years people turned left at The Plough, and now it isn't The Plough. He won't find it easy to park, either. Never is on a Sunday.'

'It will be all right,' she said. She leant across and gave him a kiss.

They heard footsteps on the front path.

'This is him,' said Dilys. 'You'd better go, Joanna.'

Dilys didn't often call her that.

Jo picked Annie up, although she was getting too big to carry, and left the room. She could see Peter through the glass. He used to press his nose right into the red lozenge shape. But today he didn't. She opened the door and said hullo. He kissed Annie, then pecked Jo on the cheek. Annie smiled and hid her face in Jo's shoulder. They stood in the doorway of the front room together, Peter slightly ahead, as Jo had manoeuvred him there. Geoff got to his feet. He and Peter shook hands and exchanged remarks on the motorway traffic. Dilys kept to her chair and bobbed her head. She had asked Jo earlier if she should offer Peter coffee and there was something about the need to ask the question and the word *offer* which made Jo say not to bother.

'You didn't bring Ella, then?' Dilys said.

'No,' said Peter. 'She stayed behind.'

He glanced round quickly, at eye level. He wouldn't have been able to describe the room ten minutes ago; he wasn't good at remembering the look of things. But Jo could see from his face that he knew that it was exactly as it used to be. He didn't want to re-learn it.

'I told you she wouldn't be coming,' Jo said. He hadn't used the Tara word.

'She might have changed her mind,' Dilys said. 'How is she?'

'She's fine,' said Peter.

Rob looked up at him.

'Oh, Rob, I didn't see you there,' he said. 'Hi.'

'Hi,' said Rob.

'It was quite a surprise when you rang this morning,' Dilys said.

She couldn't help being chatty. She'd always had a lighter touch with her grandson-in-law. The habit returned, in spite of all the things she'd said and thought about him in the last few years.

'It was too early to call you,' said Peter. 'I'm sorry, I wasn't thinking.'

'We're generally up by seven,' Dilys said. 'When I heard your voice I thought something had happened to Ella. That was the first thing I thought. I worry about her. It may be daft but I can't help it.'

'No, she's fine,' said Peter. 'I didn't mean to give you a fright.'

'Well, you said straight away there was nothing untoward. Then, when Joanna came off the phone, she said you were going to give her a lift home.'

'Yes,' he said.

'I thought you must be up in London,' Dilys said.

'I told you he wasn't,' Jo said.

Dilys glared at her and Peter looked inept.

'It's good of you to come all this way to fetch them,' Geoff said.

He sounded grateful, though Jo knew he didn't want them to leave. His remark was a reflex – some bygone male solidarity.

'You'd tell us if anything was the matter, wouldn't you?' said Dilys.

'Yes,' Peter said. 'Yes, of course.'

It was bare as a reply, but it would do. He had always colluded with Jo in fielding Dilys's interrogations, without getting any better at it. She could hear how she and her ex-husband sounded – as if they were in some kind of conspiracy. She marvelled that loyalty could be piecemeal; some aspects of it, like this, ingrained and others sent flying. He could be unfaithful and go and live with another woman. But he wouldn't call her names in front of her grandparents, or give anything away.

'You look under the weather,' said Dilys.

Peter looked as if he hadn't slept, but Dilys wouldn't put it like that. It would invoke bed and aspects of life best not drawn attention to.

'This extra driving won't do you any good,' Dilys said, 'if you're going down with something.'

'You can't rely on Sunday trains,' said Geoff. 'Engineering works. Rob got stuck last year when he came to stay with us, do you remember? He sat outside Dover Priory station for an hour and a half.'

'They could have stopped longer if they'd wanted,' said Dilys. 'They've only just arrived. I can't see what the hurry is.'

'It's easier by car,' said Geoff. 'They want to take the opportunity.'

'We'll be here again soon,' Jo said. 'I promise.'

She knew she'd compromised her grandparents. With Peter there as a third party she could hear them, circling the situation, not understanding, but unable to leave well alone. They were too decent to be false. She should never have come. She hadn't run back to them when Peter had left. She had had more sense.

When had she and Peter last been here together? She couldn't remember a particular occasion. She must have been pregnant with Annie. She hadn't known it was the last time, or the day might have stood out more clearly. Visits to East Greenwich revolved around meals and hot drinks between meals, board games and card games, turns round the garden. Peter's parents had laid on more elaborate arrangements. Trips to local beauty spots and lunches out in country places.

'Are you ready to go, Rob?' Jo said. 'We'll be leaving soon.'

She and Geoff and Peter were still standing up. Annie was heavy in her arms, but she didn't want to put her down. She used her as a shield. Annie clung on.

'Nothing to do. Done it all,' Rob said, shaking himself awake, surprised to be spoken to. He had taken himself off to some comfortable hollow where he hoped not to be disturbed until ordinary life returned. 'There's just that stuff.'

The bags were still stacked in the middle of the floor, like overnight contributions to the charity shop. The best place for them, Jo thought. Or in the back garden with a match put to them. Only she hadn't got the nerve to do it. She would have to pretend they weren't so numerous, have the family help her carry them to Peter's car, move them across the country and rediscover them at the other end.

'There's always a lot to carry with children,' said Geoff.

No one contradicted him and Annie was too little to know what was being heaped on her. Jo looked down at her. The clothes she had on could have been squashed into a mug.

'We'd better think about going,' said Peter. 'Beat the Sunday drivers.'

'That's right. There'll be plenty of them,' said Geoff. 'The forecast's good.'

Peter and Geoff began to pick up the bags. They went to

and from the car. Dilys watched them from the front window as they went up and down the short garden path. When the removal was complete the whole family ended up in the narrow hall with the door shut again. Proper hospitality demanded this.

'You look after that cut of yours,' Dilys said.

'I'm all right, Gran,' Jo said automatically. 'Don't worry about me.'

They didn't take long to leave, once they had made up their minds to go. The claustrophobic goodbyes and kind intentions in the small hallway became airborne when the door was opened.

Jo got in the car next to Peter. The kids were strapped in the back. Geoff and Dilys stood by the gate to see them off. This was how things used to be. They hadn't made much progress. Geoff waved. He always put a lot into a wave and Jo always felt sad when she saw it.

2

Knees were what you noticed, and hands, when you sat next to someone in a car. Jo had spent time looking at them only a few days ago. Felpo had to concentrate on the road, but she enjoyed sitting next to him. It never felt as if they were locked up together. This morning, in Peter's passenger seat, it was easier to stare out, rely on steady speed through the moving landscape. He had changed his car. The old one had been smaller and less plush. She did her best to be lulled, but travelling eastwards, stopping fitfully through the outer London suburbs, with the sun shining brilliantly through the glass, she had to make an effort. She looked vaguely at the houses as they peeled back, then, with more attention, at those beside the traffic lights, fated to be examined a thousand times a day. Home improvement was the only drama, windows flung open, rooms exposed like stage sets, ladders propped against walls, skips wedged against garages. Other upheavals stayed hidden.

They drew level with another family. Jo looked at them. Four heads under a low roof, the dad with his arms wrapped round the steering wheel for comfort, the mum offering none, two kids in the back, already in a trance. So they also must have appeared – no one speaking.

The road broadened into a dual carriageway. She stretched her legs, relaxed into the seat. Peter shifted slightly next to her. Speed calmed them. There would be an end to this journey. There was flat built-over land to the north, no sign of the Thames, flat bitty countryside to the south, no sign of the Downs. The traffic ahead coalesced again, channelled into a single lane. The temporary signs had an air of permanence. They were back to stopping and starting, watching brake lights, breathing in exhaust fumes through the open windows. Peter would say something soon. Free Recovery, Jo read silently, Await Rescue. Excuses formed like bubbles, overblown, then popped before she'd caught them. She had no excuses.

'Your grandparents seem well,' he said.

'Yes. They're fine, I think,' she said.

'Older, of course. But in pretty good shape,' he said.

This wasn't what she had expected. He fell silent again. More minutes passed.

'Would you ever have bothered to find out where she was?' he said.

So, that was how he'd begin. The pleasantries hadn't continued. She had guessed the tone, though not the exact words.

'What kind of question is that?' she said.

'It's a question.'

'Yes, then I would have bothered, as you say.'

'When?'

'I don't know. I told you it was no kind of question.'

She could have stopped all this by initiating what he would consider to be a grown-up conversation about Ella's welfare. She could stop it now.

'She'll be all right. I'll talk to her,' she said.

'I should bloody well think so.'

'I just said I would.'

'That's not the point, though, is it?'

Jo didn't reply.

'What are you going to say to her, then?' he said.

'I don't know. In advance.'

'You must have some idea.'

'I can't rehearse conversations like that.'

'Why not?'

'We live together.'

'What's that supposed to mean?'

'We're used to each other. I'll know what to say when I see her. Her face.'

'Pity it didn't work before.'

'What?'

'This understanding between you, based on living together.'

Jo knew she had asked for that. She said nothing. He saw in her replies a travesty of calm rationality. She knew they were based on inattention. Because his own way of talking was functional he assumed everyone else's was. She should have stuck to particular points.

Checking up on what Ella was doing every minute of the day was impossible. Peter didn't understand. He'd left when Ella had been a real child, only reaching as far as his chest. Life had been different. Jo tried to keep track of where Ella was, as if accompanying her daughter in her mind would ward off trouble, but this was superstition. Mothers weren't meant to be guardian angels. Whenever she tried to follow her daughter mentally, she failed to get past the first five minutes. She didn't know where to put herself. Whether to be a shadow tagging along behind, or to be herself, pretending to be Ella. It was simpler to keep Ella at the back of her mind, then, when she wasn't where she had said she'd be, or too much time had elapsed, to trouble herself with inflammatory images. The car spinning off the road, the hands round the throat, the tide coming in too fast. This was what passed for concern, love even. It was the way mothers thought.

Since Friday, she had lost the will to think.

The traffic from the opposite carriageway was cutting across on the diagonal. A lorry swayed past them, a looming shape blocking the light. Jo flinched.

'What did you do that for?' asked Peter.

'I didn't mean to. I thought the lorry was going to hit us,' she said.

In a moment they would be through the road-works. There it was – Free Recovery At An End. The oncoming cars were safe back on their own side. Peter put on speed again, but the trick didn't work a second time.

'So this fellow's gone for good, has he? He won't be living with you.' Peter paused between the words in the wrong places. He was embarrassed.

'I wouldn't have thought so. I don't know,' she said.

'So you might still see him?'

'Probably not,' she said.

'What does it depend on?'

'I don't know. Whether he's around or not, for a start. He won't be. I don't expect he will be.'

'You could decide not to see him. Couldn't you? Or is that beyond you?'

Jo said nothing.

'Have you gone stupid or something?'

'That sort of thing.'

She undid her seat belt.

'What are you doing?' he said.

'Nothing.'

'I thought you were going to jump out.'

'The family failing. No. I couldn't breathe.'

She snapped the fastening shut again.

'He's violent,' he said.

'He isn't. Once. That was all.'

'That's enough, isn't it?'

'Yes. Yes it is.'

'You're contradicting yourself.'

'Yes. It happens.'

'I need something more positive than this from you.'

'OK,' she said.

'The kids are in the back,' he said.

'I realise.'

148

'So, I'm being careful what I say. Don't take advantage of that.'

Their children were entirely silent. Annie either asleep or listening in that intent way that small children do. The dissonance repels and attracts them. The uneven speech and threadbare intervals. They're able to reproduce them perfectly themselves in later life. Rob would be trying not to hear, trusting that at some point the conversation would end, convinced his own adult life would be saner. Jo hoped for his sake it would be. She didn't turn round to look at him.

'You were frightened when it happened. Admit it. You ran away from him. Back to Geoff and Dilys,' Peter said.

'Thanks. It was a mistake. I didn't think about what I was doing.'

'And you are doing now?'

'No. I don't know. I've already said I don't know.'

Only once she had said, as though isolated cases had immunity. She guessed, though she couldn't be sure, that there was a difference between the piling up of fear and its sudden impact. It had been so quick. There had been no time to adjust. She had said so few words to Felpo – but that moment had been her chance. It could have gone either way. People said that sometimes. Either way. She should have laughed as if she meant it. He'd have seen it too. They would both have laughed. They could be laughing now. She should have been angry. I-can't-believe-what's-happening. Yelling, running all the words together. They were quite similar, laughing and shouting. They required energy and noise. She hadn't managed either response. She and Felpo hadn't been used to falling out. Those patterns in which, after five minutes' injection of new material, she says what she said last time and he says what he said last time – the familiar pitching which ends more often in faintly nauseous sleep than in plunging over the side – they hadn't even begun to form, they were years away. They had been too close to be of use to each other.

Peter had hit her once. He'd grabbed her right hand and held it tight while he slapped her arm. That was well before Tara. It had happened near the beginning of their marriage. She couldn't remember what the row had been about but she could remember exactly where she had been standing. Next to the bath in the bathroom of their old house. There had been a lot of wet washing hanging over a rack. Surely the row couldn't have been about washing? Perhaps she had shrunk something or the colours had run. She had hit him back.

'What do you want to do when we get there?' Peter said.

His voice was different. He was trying. She would try too. 'I don't mind.'

She hesitated. 'There' had no meaning. It had vanished. She had always liked getting home after being away, carrying on with the present after a shot of something different which was already the past. Now she had to concentrate to remind herself what home was.

For a while they were silent.

'Have you been on holiday yet? You went to Spain in September last year, didn't you?' she asked.

He didn't reply straight away. 'I thought we were talking about making arrangements,' he said.

'Sorry. Yes, we were. What are the choices?'

He took his eyes off the road for a second and looked at her. You don't have to look at someone's face if you're driving and up till now he hadn't. He looked ahead again.

'I think it would be best if I took Rob and Annie home with me,' he said. 'Then dropped you off with all your stuff and made sure everything was all right.'

'What do you mean, all my stuff?'

'All your bags. In the boot.'

'Oh, them. Yes. I'd forgotten about them.'

Jo could see them cluttering up the pavement, but nothing

behind them. An infinite stretch of paving, without a house in sight.

'You've worked it all out then?' she said. 'What we should do?'

'It was a suggestion. You don't have to agree. There's no need to be touchy.'

'I just wondered what was the point of asking, if you've worked it all out.'

He didn't reply.

'Was it witches who had to choose their own punishment?' she said. 'They could say whether they preferred to be burned or drowned? I'm sure I've read that somewhere.'

'I don't know. It was a test, wasn't it? Is that what you're thinking of?'

'Could be,' she said.

'If they stuck the witch in water and she survived, it showed she was a witch. If she drowned, they knew she must have been normal,' he said. 'No, that can't be it.'

It seemed likely enough, Jo thought.

'What made you think of that?' he said.

'I was thinking about choices. I thought we were talking about them.'

He seemed to take a slow breath.

'Is your back hurting?' she asked.

'No, it's fine. Why?'

'You used to get backache from driving.'

'Tension, probably,' he said.

'What did you mean, make sure everything's all right?' she said.

'It's obvious, isn't it?'

'Is it?'

'For God's sake, Jo.'

'Leave her alone, Dad,' Rob said, suddenly. 'Mum, do you want to stop? We can stop. Or we can go back to Gran's.'

'Christ Almighty,' said Peter. 'What is all this? Believe me, we are not going back anywhere.'

Jo could only see the surface of the road. Her feet were pulled along it. She was on the train again, but too close to the rails. There was no floor but the train was moving, the metal passing suavely on both sides, the wooden sleepers flicking by underneath her.

'Mum. Are you OK?' The voice came from very far away.

She took a deep breath and closed her eyes. When she opened them, the road was outside again.

'It's all right, Rob,' she said. 'We'll go on.'

Having parked the car, Peter came up to the flat with her, Rob and Annie tagged behind. When they got to the small landing at the top of the stairs Jo realised that the place was banal and empty, at peace with itself. She noticed Peter's fists relax as soon as he got inside. He hesitated, listening, but there was nothing to hear but the household sounds of the kitchen clock and the fridge working hard in the heat. Perhaps he'd expected blood on the walls. He seemed to be staring at them. Two of her drawings, dog-eared at the corners, were pinned next to the calendar. One was of a pair of glass candlesticks standing one behind the other, the second of the stairs rising up through the shop. Peter asked if Ella had done them and Rob said, no, they were Mum's. Peter said they were interesting; she should do more of that sort of thing. Jo shook her head.

Rob said he'd stay at home with her, but Jo didn't encourage him. She said that she was going to go to sleep and all three of them – even Annie – looked at her as if she were in a hospital bed. Perhaps she had said it too wearily. Then they said goodbye, glad that visiting time was over. She heard Annie minutes later in the street outside, talking, happy. They drove off with all the bags in the car with them. That was tactful. The flat was as tidy as a desert. Jo had never seen it look like that. She couldn't remember having cleared up on Friday afternoon. Everything was washed up and put away, Annie's toys out of sight, the rubbish put out. It would have smelled in the heat. The assortment of chairs, squared-up round the table, looked across at each other like difficult guests. The windows had been left slightly open, top and bottom, and two of the main lights were still on. Sixty watts outshone by daylight. Jo didn't switch them off. She wandered round the rooms looking for other signs of previous occupancy, but found none. Nothing extra in the fridge, nothing taken out of it, the bed properly made, the towels dry in the bathroom. He must have been back, though, because his things weren't there – nothing. What remained, her own belongings, she looked at with hostility.

The unacceptable dead and lost, where do you put them, she wondered. She couldn't remember anyone owning up to the unacceptable dead, though there were plenty of them. Far more than the living equivalent. Death did the necessary, and people stopped complaining about the deceased's defects. Into the Book of Remembrance they went, along with the honourable ones. The crematorium calligrapher wasn't asked to use an identifying script. Gail Price it said. Nicely inscribed, like an A-level certificate. On the same page were other names. Reginald Longley, she remembered. It had rolled off the tongue. Her father – though father seemed the wrong word for a boy of eighteen – hadn't been in the book. They used to go to the crematorium chapel twice a year. On the anniversary of the death and on Gail's birthday. But the book was only open on the anniversary. She had had to wear a skirt and proper shoes.

The unacceptable lost weren't allowed the same kind treatment. Unlike the dead, they might come back, so it was best to take the opportunity to run them down and try to put off anyone obtuse enough to have loved them. She would realise that she was better off without him. Peter had said that to her on the telephone. At least the bad ending to her love affair spared her sympathy. Those platitudes about time. As if time were ever available in advance. It was easier to manipulate distance. If Felpo had crossed the Channel on Friday evening and kept driving, he'd be over several borders by now. Greece or Hungary – Lake Balaton. He said he'd like to go there. There wouldn't be too many hold-ups. The crowds would all be running in the other direction, back with their tanned faces and damp laundry. She had no reason to imagine him at maximum miles away in relation to hours, but that is where she put him. If he were any closer she wouldn't be able to cope.

He hadn't brought much with him when he moved in. His clothes came in a couple of rucksacks. Everything else had stayed in the van. He had paid the rent on his previous place until the end of the month but he let another tenant take it with money still on the clock. It had been depressing, he said – a ground-floor room in Folkestone hemmed in by the backs of restaurants with nothing to look out on but extractor fan outlets and steamed-up windows. He hadn't taken Jo to see it.

She opened the kitchen drawer in case anything of his had found its way there. She saw knives and spatulas and wooden spoons passed on by Dilys or bought from Woolworth's, two corkscrews – one bought in a petrol station for an evening picnic – a bottle opener from Snowdonia, old crumbs and a hair – her own. She took the lid off the kettle. The water had been there since Friday, or looked as if it had. A few inches with a rainbow film on the surface. She caught herself staring at it. She thought, knowing whether or not he had made himself a cup of tea added nothing to wisdom. She tipped the water out quickly. No one ever came back for standing water.

She left the kitchen and went to bed – Ella's. She couldn't face her own. It was hardly midday, so lying down didn't even count as an afternoon nap. Ella's room was different from the rest of the flat. Lengths of dark cloth tacked to the walls. Clothes heaped in piles. It was like being in a patchwork tent that had been wrongly put up, with surplus swathes lying on the floor. Jo didn't mind about mess any more. Outside it was still Sunday. Cars went by making their purposeless Sunday drone. She slept on and off through the rest of the day and the following night, getting up only to pee and drink water, crawling back under Ella's bedclothes. Her arms and legs lay at difficult angles. Without Felpo to fit into she couldn't make them agree. She hadn't missed him in that way on the front-room sofa. In a real bed again, she felt his absence. She gave up trying to find comfort and put her face further into the pillow, smelling Ella's sweetish smell buried inside.

He had attacked her. To Peter and Tara, to her grandparents – had they known the story – Felpo's sudden aggression would have been believable as well as true. No further explanation was necessary. But she couldn't find one. They had loved each other, but jealousy hadn't been part of love. He had said 'Of course' when she had said Trevor was on the phone. That was all she had to go on.

3

Although they had all finished eating, the wasps wouldn't leave them alone. They liked the tomato pips that had squirted on to the table and the sweet wet rings left by the glasses. They smelled the salty crumbs of potato crisps on Annie's fingers. Years ago wasps used to fly round plum trees but now they were scavengers addicted to ready meals. They walked sideways along the joins in the picnic table and then buzzed out to eat. There was a large ashtray in front of Ella and, in her bag, one cigarette. She wanted it but she couldn't have it, so, to distract herself, she observed a wasp. She chose one in particular, and watched it edge its way through the shadows between the wooden slats – cunningly aiming too deep to be whacked. It got as far as the hole that was meant for umbrellas and fizzed about in the round space, getting excitable.

They were sitting in a pub yard having an early supper. Peter, Annie and Rob on one of the benches, Tara and Ella facing them on the other. It was a town pub on a street corner. There were no flowers or trees or umbrellas, but if you went inside the pub to the toilet, the door that you came back out of said Garden. Over the fence there was a real one with a lawn and a greenhouse and a swing seat. The owners were busy – a woman wielding a green hose, showering a border of roses with light spray, and a man trimming a hedge. Ella could hear that they were still there – the water swooshing, the shears whispering and clicking in regular rhythm. But she was observing the wasp.

There had been too much talking. Peter and Tara on the way back from the ferry terminal last night. Tara on her bed this morning. Tara while they were waiting for Peter to come back from London. They'd asked too many questions and because she was never going to lie again, she had replied. She had got sick of replying – but she hadn't offered any extra information. Phil Phelps she'd called him. She'd had enough of Felpo. When Peter arrived with Rob and Annie they had changed the subject and talked of other things.

Rob had hardly said anything. He had sat as far away from her as he could and watched television. Sometimes he'd looked at her. He'd looked at Tara's white towelling dressing gown as if to say, so that's what you wear now, is it? Peter had tried to get a family discussion going about where they should go out to eat, but only he and Tara took part. Tara said that some place in a wood, miles away, was under new management and Peter said that it was a long time since he'd had a pizza. It wasn't really an argument but they carried on with it for about an hour. Ella had tried smiling at Rob, just a small smile, but he had ignored her. In the end they had walked down the hill to the pub. Tara had carried a shawl thing to sit on because she was wearing cream-coloured jeans.

'That won't be allowed next week,' Peter said.

'What's that, darling?' Tara said.

'Watering. The hosepipe ban will come into force if we don't get any rain.'

'It won't affect us,' Tara said. 'Thank God for decking.'

'You have to pay a supplement to the water rates if you have a sprinkler. I looked into it.'

'Did you? I thought you were all for getting rid of that tatty greenery.'

'I was.'

Tara yawned. 'Oh. Sorry, everyone,' she said.

'I'm feeling a bit like that myself,' Peter said. 'We'd better all have an early one. How was the All Day Breakfast, Rob?'

'Good,' Rob said.

'Let's have a dessert. Did anyone look at the board?' Peter said.

'Pass,' Tara said.

'Rob?' Peter said.

'Don't know,' Rob said. 'Didn't see a board.'

'Does anyone else fancy sticky toffee pudding? I'm having that if they've got any,' Peter said.

'Peter,' Tara said.

'What?' Peter said.

'No,' Tara said.

'Oh, all right,' Peter said. 'Just testing. No takers for dessert then. What about Annie? How about an ice cream?'

The wasp had stopped fizzing in the hole and had started to bob across the table. Ella bent down, so that her eyes were level with the surface. On the far side was a glass smeared yellow with orange juice and Annie's hands either side, looking blurry and larger than life-size. There were two wasps now and Ella had to concentrate to make sure she had the right one. She wanted to know whether her wasp was touching the surface. It appeared to be, but if it really were, wouldn't it start fizzing again? It moved in jerky patterns so it was hard to track, but, she thought, in general, it missed by a whisker every time. Then, without warning, the background to the investigation broke up. Annie's hands shot in the air and the glass toppled and rolled towards Ella. Her wasp took off.

'Look what you've done,' she said.

'Look what *you've* done, you arsehole,' Rob shouted.

'Rob, pipe down. Annie, what is the matter?' Peter said.

Annie was wailing and sucking her hand.

'It was your fault. You made it sting her,' Rob said.

'I didn't,' Ella said.

'You did. I was watching you. You sent it over. You *willed* it over.'

'You're just thick. How did I will it?' She climbed out of the bench and stood up. 'Just tell me, how did I will it?'

'Ella, sit down,' Peter said.

'You out-stared it,' Rob said. 'Animals don't like that. Not from someone with an evil face like yours. Fucking troublemaker.'

'Say that again,' Ella said.

'Rob,' Peter said.

'Fucking troublemaker,' Rob said.

'Ella, stay where you are,' Peter said.

She took no notice. She had already shot round to the other side of the table and was pummelling Rob's head. He put his arms up to shield himself and then she moved on to his shoulders, one hand on each, forcing his forehead down on to the table, kneeing him in the back. He resisted. She increased the pressure. Peter shouted at her to cut it. She felt him come up behind her and grasp her arms above the elbow, enough to hurt. She struggled. He heaved. He was bigger than she was but not as angry. She carried on pushing downwards – fighting against the force that was pulling her backwards – but she lost her advantage and Rob took the opportunity to slither out of her grasp and crawl under the table.

'Let go of me,' she said, shaking loose.

Peter released her. He was out of breath.

'Jesus,' he said. 'What have I done to deserve this family?'

'Cow,' Rob said, as he emerged on the opposite bench, next to Tara.

Annie climbed down from the bench and tugged at Peter's arm.

'I wasn't stinged,' she said.

4

Jo slept from five until eight, when she was disturbed. The front door banged and, after a few minutes, the motorbike belonging to the downstairs neighbours revved up and went. She turned over and opened her eyes. A high and uncrossable wall had gone up since she had last heard that noise. She couldn't get back there. Part of her, though, wasn't sorry to be home. After Dilys's – after years of family life – the flat was a blank space. When had she last woken up alone in a house? She had gained time to herself by frightening them all away – though she didn't know what use to put it to. She got out of bed. Even putting her feet to the floor was a strange experiment. A bee bumped into the window. No other sounds. She went into the passage. Through the kitchen door she could see a glass half-full of water on the draining board together with the packet of painkillers that she must have taken in the middle of the night. Careless to have left them there, she thought. Then she remembered that Annie wasn't at home. She sat down at the table with her head resting in her hands. She knew he would be gone, not just him, but anything of him. There was nothing there on the outside. She had never known anyone so thoroughly missing. They'd expect her to get to work on the inside too, scouring him out. They kept away and hoped she would recover with a dose of her own solitude. But she didn't know how to administer it, nor where to begin.

They came back in a rush, pounding up the stairs, filling the room. Peter in his shirtsleeves, but with a tie on, dressed for work, Ella, Rob and Annie with their summer arms and legs. They stood on the other side of the kitchen and gave Jo the same look. Their expressions were related. She didn't often see that. She smiled at them and pushed her chair away from the table.

'Did you have a good time yesterday?' she asked.

'Yes, we had fun, didn't we?' Peter said, turning to include the kids. 'We went out to eat in the evening. Just to the pub down the road. Picnic tables, child-friendly. You know the sort of thing. Ella didn't want to go anywhere by car.'

'You and Tara did?' Jo said.

'We'd thought about going somewhere inland with more atmosphere. But it turned out all right,' he said.

'Annie got a splinter,' Rob said.

'Did you, Annie? Show me,' Jo said.

Annie held both hands out. She hated splinters. She rubbed her hands over any grey and grainy-looking wood until she was sure she wouldn't get one. Jo always carried a packet of needles with her. It was no good telling her.

'I can't see anything,' Jo said. 'It must be better.'

'It was all a bit of a pantomime but I won't go into it now,' Peter said.

'Fine,' Jo said.

'We've brought some of the bags up,' Peter said. 'They're on the landing. I'll go and get the rest.'

'Don't worry,' Jo said. 'You'll be late getting to work. I'll come down.'

'Like that?' he said.

She looked down at herself, surprised. Yesterday's T-shirt and skirt. She'd worn them in bed. She smoothed down the skirt.

'Yes,' she said.

She followed him down the stairs and into the hallway.

Megan, the downstairs neighbour, was letting herself in. She must be taking the day off work, Jo thought. She smiled and Megan smiled back. She found it restful that they didn't say hello – and somehow more intimate, though they knew nothing about each other.

She and Peter went out into the street. He unlocked the boot of the car and leant inside for the battered holdall and the plastic laundry bag with its handles tied together. He put them on the ground.

'Leave them there,' she said. 'I'll manage.'

'You'll be all right?'

'You've done most of it,' she said.

'I meant, in general.'

'Yes, I'll be all right,' she said. 'Thanks for helping out.'

'Ella seems to be calmer,' he said.

'I'm glad.'

'Tara had a good talk with her yesterday morning. It might have made it easier for you, paved the way,' he said.

'Yes,' she said.

'She'll need time to recover. Tara would talk to her again, if you wanted her to. She's sympathetic. She seems to understand what she's been through.'

'Once is probably fine,' Jo said.

'She did her best. So did I. You didn't see Ella, last night, down at the ferry terminal. Sitting in the cafe´ there, in the middle of the night. That kind bloke had picked her up – a total stranger. Christ, we were lucky.'

'Yes,' Jo said. 'She was lucky too.'

'Has she really no idea how dangerous it is to take lifts?'

'She knows,' Jo said. She paused. 'I'm glad the man who gave her the lift didn't tell her. She probably wouldn't have agreed to use his mobile to call you.'

'She was a mess. Crying, shivering. I've never seen her like that.'

Neither of them spoke.

'She was crying when you found her?' Jo said.

'No. When she saw me. Relief, I suppose. I was bloody relieved too.'

Jo nodded. 'What happened to the man?' she said.

'He had to leave to catch the ferry. He had a wedding to get to. He left her in the care of the café attendant. I thanked the woman, of course. She made light of it all. Said she didn't know what I was talking about. I'd like to get hold of the fellow's address. Send him a crate of wine or something.'

Jo imagined the man on his own again after his encounter with Ella. She saw him flicking through his travel documents, leaning across to the left-hand side of the windscreen, maybe re-sticking a loose corner of his tax disc, driving up the ramp to the car deck. Peter used to do those things. Before the ferry sailed he might have looked back and seen the girl and her father in miniature before they disappeared from the terminal buildings.

Peter was prodding the near tyre with his foot, as if gauging the pressure.

'She was frightened of him,' he said. 'That's why she jumped off the train. She saw him.'

'She told you that?' Jo knew who *him* was.

'More or less. Well, I needed some explanation.'

'That's probably why she gave you one,' she said.

'She wasn't lying,' he said.

'No? Though she might, if pushed – like most people,' she said.

'Then she thought she saw him at the Sandrock Hotel,' he said.

'Thought?'

'He wasn't actually there. She was in such a state. Does it matter?'

She shook her head.

'What was she doing at the Sandrock Hotel?' she said.

'With someone called Vince, apparently. She has too much freedom.'

'He's nice, isn't he? Vince. Have you met him? She may not realise how nice. Weird place for them to go.'

'What exactly is their relationship?'

He said it as he used to say to her, Why did you leave those tomatoes rotting in the fridge, or, Why did you leave the skylight open in the rain? She hadn't known then and she didn't know now. She could have said that Vince was a year younger than Ella and that Ella didn't fancy him, which would have kept Peter quiet but been a cop-out – not fair to anyone. He seemed to know that she wasn't going to reply.

'Then the evening before she was out with Trevor. Anything to get out of the flat, she said. That's no good, Jo.'

'You seem to have found out a lot.'

'I made it my business to find out. I wanted a picture of her activities.'

'I see.'

'Have you got any plans?' Peter asked. This sounded less personal, a form of goodbye. He would leave soon.

She replied in the same manner, 'There are always things to do. No plans.'

'You haven't come to any decisions?' he said.

She sighed loudly enough for him to hear. It wasn't enough to be in one piece today. She had to promise to be in one piece tomorrow as well, having made New Year resolutions. They had had similar exchanges over the years, a whole clutch of them at the time of his leaving. She had never managed reassurances about uncertainties; they seemed as unconvincing as a horoscope. What Peter wanted for her was monotony, gingered up with graspable events – short breaks, days out, birthdays, Christmases. He'd call it happiness probably, as long as she could afford it. And if the worst happened – for instance, falling in love with an unsuitable person, which would score about the same as being in a road accident, or being attacked by your unsuitable lover, which would be the same as going through the windscreen – then the best you could do would be to carry on as if it had never

164

happened, organising short breaks, days out, birthdays, Christmases . . .

Ella had jumped; it was brave to jump. Jo hoped, for her sake, it had been as free as it looked.

'She thought she heard him upstairs at Lois Lucas's,' Peter said. 'She thought he was there, waiting in the bedroom. That's why she ran out. It sounded like some sort of panic attack.' He shook his head. 'One and a half nights she spent in that shop.'

'He wouldn't have been there, whatever you and Tara think,' Jo said. 'Why would he go to Lois Lucas's at that time of night? Nothing about it makes sense.'

'She said she thought he was waiting for you,' he said.

'In Trevor's bedroom? What's that supposed to be about?'

As she spoke, she felt a vague disturbance in her head that was more like the pressure of unequal weights behind her eyes than real pain.

'That's what she said. It doesn't make sense, I agree. Why would you be there in the middle of the night?' he said.

She smiled hazily, as if she'd discerned the source of a gas leak.

'Thank you for telling me. You needn't have. Did she tell you what exactly she was frightened of?' she said.

'No, and I didn't push it,' he said.

He looked at his watch. Jo had no idea what time it was.

'We're not getting anywhere,' she said. 'Let's forget it. I'll give Tara a call. Thank her for her help.'

He looked astonished. 'You don't have to.'

'I'd like to. There's probably some truth in what she's been saying.'

'What has she been saying?'

She laughed. 'I can guess,' she said. 'I'll be fine. You go.'

He pointed the car keys at the car and the locks clicked – the usual anti-climax.

She watched him drive away and went back indoors.

Inside the hall, the door to the left was propped wide open and Jo could see right through the house to her neighbours' garden. Cooler it looked down there, smelling of clean washing – the patch of outdoors at the far end, a dark August green. They could perhaps swap, she and the neighbours. Even at this late stage, she could change her mind and choose downstairs. Wear the smaller size of the trainers neatly lined up in pairs on the tiles, take the video lying next to them back to the video shop, peg out the clothes on the line. They seemed to have a simple life – orderly. They had a fuzzy inside to their letterbox and a special holder for milk bottles.

After the move, she would hear them walking about above her. She would know the lay-out and where their feet were going. They would go diagonally across the floor at night and then stop. There was only one possible place for a double bed, with the head on the inside wall where the fireplace used to be. She wondered if they would pray before they got into it. She had always thought of them as the Christian couple but she had no evidence for so naming them apart from the text on the back of the bike. The Kingdom of God is Within You. Perhaps that was all there was to it. Dilys had always told her that Gail was in heaven, but the fact – since it was presented as such – seemed irrelevant. Gail wasn't here and that was what counted. Jo was as certain as she could be that there was no such thing as a soul – but she didn't rule out the possibility of losing one.

In the evenings, her new old neighbours, Dan and Megan, would bang about in her former flat in a discreet way, hoovering, knocking brooms into corners, painting over the stains. She would give them time to get straight and then, in a hospitable way, she would ask them down. They would have cups of tea in the garden. Annie would hand round biscuits on plates. She knew the sort of person she would be if she lived downstairs. Living where Dan and Megan used to live. Knowing they were above her, setting things to rights. She knew intensely, there was nothing vague about it.

In the garden a tap was turned on and water splashed into a watering can. Jo moved away out of sight and pushed open her own door. She took her time over climbing the stairs.

She had long ago given up working out what she was going to say in advance, even beginnings. Sentences she planned – though they started out neutral – acidulated while they were waiting, good for nothing when the time came. Dilys always prepared difficult conversations to audition pitch, not just her part, but the other person's as well. The advantage of this method was that when you said something different from what she had expected, she carried straight on as if no one had spoken. On the receiving end, you felt not so much misunderstood as bypassed. Peter retrieved signpost phrases from Tara. He liked contemporary clichés; they seemed livelier than his own. When he finally got round to telling Jo about Tara – it had been at the bottle bank at three o'clock on a Sunday afternoon – they had dropped into his confession like globs of oil on water, unassimilated.

Jo had told Peter that she would know what to say when she saw Ella's face and she still hoped she would.

Ella was sitting at the kitchen table, sharpening coloured pencils for Annie, taking care over them so that the shavings fell on to a piece of white paper in perfect spirals. Annie was drawing at the opposite end. Rob was up in his room.

'Did Rob manage to eat anything yesterday?' Jo said. 'Gran over-fed us as usual.'

'Dad said, "How's the All Day Breakfast, Rob?" So I suppose he was eating. I didn't look to see.'

Ella blew the dust from the sharpening into a tiny pile.

'He says interesting things, your dad,' Jo said.

'Earlier he said next Sunday was only a week away.'

'That was for Annie's benefit, was it?' Jo said.

'No, Tara's.'

'She'd lost track of time?'

'She kept saying she couldn't believe she hadn't read the Sundays yet, she could do with having the weekend over again.'

'Why couldn't she read them?' Jo said.

'I don't know. Too geed up.'

'Was she? Peter said she'd had a heart-to-heart with you.'

The hair to the left of Ella's parting was tucked behind her ear. To the right it fell down and brushed the paper and hid her from view. She still hadn't looked up.

'Is that what he called it?' Ella said.

'Wasn't that what it was?' Jo said.

'Like with a nice WPC. She sat on the bed this morning and wouldn't let me pretend to go back to sleep. Every time she moved I thought, she'll get up now, but she didn't, she just pulled the sheet tighter.'

'She talked, though?'

Ella raised her eyes from the pencils and gazed up at the grubby line where the walls met the ceiling and the spiders lived. Her face shone with enthusiasm.

'"I like this room. Don't you? White's so calming,"' she said.

'Doesn't sound too controversial. Do WPCs say that?' Jo said.

'"I said to Peter after you'd gone to bed, 'She's in shock,' but he said, 'She's caught cold.' Shock isn't even an emotion," she said, "There's no need for him to be so squeamish about it.'"

Jo smiled. Ella did the voice well, slightly exaggerated but entirely recognisable.

"'Talk if you want to. I remember myself at your age, as if it were yesterday,'" Ella said.

'Did you?' Jo said.

The animation went from Ella's face and she carried on with the sharpening. She'd got to Annie's favourite colours that were just stubs. Blue for sky and red for houses.

'What do you think?' she said.

'What else did she say?' Jo said.

'Oh, all this stuff about me.'

Ella wouldn't tell her that. Even if she remembered word for word, she wouldn't get into the part. She'd have told her Tara's other stories. Marcia, at the office, whose hair got caught in the electric fan, or the ex-boyfriend her sister found under the bed. She had told Jo before. The rotating hair, Marcia's taut scalp. The soles of the boyfriend's boots caked in mud and dead leaves, the same leaves that were all over her sister's back garden. In Ella's case, Tara wouldn't have got the story right.

'It's no good people telling you bits of your life back to you,' Jo said. 'It never works.'

'No,' Ella said. 'They do it when they're telling you off and they do it to cosy up to you.'

Jo wasn't going to do either. There was no point in making Ella repeat the lies, airing them like second-hand clothes. The smell never quite goes. If it hadn't been those particular lies it would have been others. These things find casual substitutes. In the half hour since Peter had left a sense of recognition, hardly different from resignation, had been growing in her, in spite of the shock. The barrier between knowing and not knowing had been as thin as skin. A few words had broken it.

She thought back to Friday. The gap between Ella leaving

the flat and Felpo coming back. They must have met by chance. Ella wouldn't have gone looking for him. The next time Jo saw Ella was when she was holding her head, pulling strands of hair off her face, tying them back in again. Rob had been there, running the tap, dabbing her cheek with cotton wool, letting water trickle down her neck, opening a bottle of antiseptic, stinging her with it. They had sat her down, pressed her head between her knees. Afterwards, when she was clearly going to live and the first shock was over, Rob had started to ask questions and Ella had told him to shut up. She had been different – not kind any more. Cold and irritable.

'Did Tara say anything about me?' Jo said.

Her daughter looked at her then, her expression bland, but spiked with something. Jo couldn't tell whether it came from Ella, or from Ella being Tara. She watched as Ella got up from the table, went to the window and leant her hands on the glass. She wasn't the one who cleaned them.

'"I don't mean to criticise her, but she should never have had him in the place with you kids there, especially you, Ella, an attractive girl. Well, you are. She should have had more respect. I appreciate some women might find it exciting, but there are limits. She should be giving you advice about sex, not having it,"' Ella said.

'She said that?'

'Yes. She said it was just an observation.'

'What advice? What advice am I supposed to be giving you?' Jo said.

Ella shrugged her shoulders.

'If you're wearing a tight skirt,' Jo said, 'take it right off, don't hitch it up. I can't think of anything else. It doesn't get clearer.'

'No,' Ella said. She didn't turn round.

'Come on, Annie. Let's get those bags unpacked. Tip them all out over my bedroom floor,' Jo said.

Her younger daughter had been sitting at the table

drawing a picture. It was a house; it always was, with fierce smoke coming out of a chimney. Funny how children put in the smoke. They'd probably be doing it in another hundred years. Annie was still little enough to be talked in front of – up to a point, anyway. If you talk rapidly and unemotionally and smile from time to time, children don't take much notice, Jo thought. She wasn't totally convinced – but some things are more important than others. She couldn't worry about Annie's ears, as well as the rest.

6

Trevor shut the shop at a quarter to five on Monday and
went across to the Co-op. A bell rang when he opened the
door and he was hit by the lack-lustre grocery smell of
smoked bacon and cheap currant buns.

'Good afternoon, Kathleen,' he said.

'Good afternoon, Mr Lucas. Hot enough for you? I see
you sitting in the sun over there but if it don't rain soon
you'll be down at the stand-pipe with your bucket.'

'Right you are, Kathleen.'

It was best to get the greetings out of the way. Kathleen
sat at the check-out, facing outwards, remembering her days
at the scrubbed marble counter. She was, as far as he knew,
the only person in East Kent who still had a rural accent, but
he distrusted it. He was looking for starch. His shirts were
limp, not soft to touch, but limp, and threadbare round the
collars and cuffs. He recalled that Lois set store by starch and
used it to titivate the old pillowcases and table linen before
putting them on display. He was sure it came in a packet but
here it was in a giant aerosol. He held the canister out at
arm's length so he could read the writing on it.

'You buying that for wasps, Mr Lucas?' Kathleen said.

'Not that I know of,' he said.

She seized the can from him and passed it over the
scanner.

'Plenty about. That's what I use it for. That'll be three
fifty-nine.'

He dug deep into his pocket and came up with a fistful of change and counted it out. The daylight robbery seemed less glaring if he didn't part with a note.

'Reckon you're the last customer, Mr Lucas?'

'I see no others, Kathleen. But there's time yet. Someone out there may, at this very moment, begin to crave an individual fruit pie.'

Kathleen snorted and fished out a bundle of keys from under the counter. Trevor left before she pursued him with the stool that she needed to stand on to draw the top bolt. He crossed the road and got into his car. He put his Co-op bag on the floor and opened all the windows. The steering wheel was burning hot and he waited for it to cool down. He thought it was a pity there wasn't some method of driving with the doors propped open – a motoring equivalent of the brick in the knitted cover he used for the shop.

He had told Jo he would pick her up some time after five. He'd rung her to find out if she was all right and she'd asked him if he'd mind driving her somewhere. He'd said, did she have anywhere particular in mind – Birmingham or Broadstairs? It was all the same to him, but he might need to re-plan his evening. She said that what she wanted to do wouldn't take long.

He had half a mind to drop in on Frankie again later. He'd been calling her that in his head – he'd have to try it out on her. Francesca was too long-winded for his liking. Where she came from the name was probably merely Catholic. He'd gone round to Borrowdale again last night, taking a couple of bottles of Cabernet Sauvignon with him. They'd taken two of Matron's wine glasses out of the cabinet. Frankie had sipped the wine in a ladylike way, holding the glass by the stem, but he noticed she downed it pretty fast, almost keeping pace with him. He liked that in a woman, though there was a cost implication. He said he was sorry about yesterday and she said she hoped he had had a good journey home. Sip, sip. Her English was sometimes rather formal. She said she had telephoned him to see if he had got back safely but there had been no reply. She had been worried about him. He was touched by that. She was prettier at a distance than close to, so he carried on talking to her without drawing nearer, enjoying her smooth, tragic face and the way she crossed her knees. He sat in Matron's armchair and she sat on the day bed. She told him of her troubles with the bank and the Benefits Agency and the Home Office. In his younger days there seemed to be a bit of a story attached to a woman, he generally came in on the tail end of it. Now women had problems. These were harder to respond to than a story. He took his hat off to them for understanding what they were talking about. He certainly didn't. The old ones down the corridors had been peaceful. They hadn't competed with him for Frankie's attentions. He had moved on to the day bed and given her a cuddle. She smelled nice. Her head fitted between his chin and his collar-bone and she had put both legs over his. He might even have drifted off himself at one point. He had enjoyed the evening and left while they were both feeling benign about each other and before either of them expected anything.

7

The wheels of Trevor's car crunched on the chalk and displaced surface dust. The dust settled on the windscreen. The coastguard station was one of the only places where the road came near the cliff edge. Sometimes there were two or three cars parked there but today they were on their own. The car windows were already wound down. Jo could hear the amplified voice giving out announcements on a cross-Channel ferry. She couldn't distinguish the words, just the rise and fall of the voice, then the warning signals for practice. The passengers would be setting out deckchairs to catch the last of the sun, forgetting that the boat turned in the harbour and they would be in the shade.

'Great view of the Channel,' said Trevor.

'I know we haven't come for the ride,' she said. 'No need to go on about it. It's good of you to drive me round scenic Kent. Especially as it's pointless.'

'Don't worry,' he said, 'I do it myself all the time. Lose things and look for them.'

He turned the radio on and stuck his elbow out of the window.

She had asked Trevor to take her to Felpo's old address in Folkestone. She had told him that Felpo had gone. Sorry to hear that, he'd said. She had knocked at the house while Trevor waited outside in the car on a double yellow line. A man had opened the door to her. She had stood on the step and Trevor had kept an eye. That's how he put it. The man had scratched his chest. He'd never heard of anyone called Felpo. Where's he from, then, he said. A woman from the restaurant next door had come out and emptied a bucket of hot dirty water into the gutter. Then, when Jo got back into the car, she had asked Trevor to drive round the country lanes for a while. He didn't mention Ella camping in the shop and she didn't say anything about the thin discoloured line down her face.

'Anything else the matter?' he said.

Jo shook her head in a vague way. Then she said, 'I met my neighbour, Megan, on the way out. She asked where the van was. She looked so pleased when I said it wouldn't be coming back.'

Trevor nodded. 'Sounds normal,' he said.

'She's obviously spent the last six months hoping that it would go. I hadn't realised she hated it so much,' she said.

'Don't worry about it,' he said. 'She wouldn't have wanted an accident, just a failed MOT – something like that.'

She stared at the sea. He was being patient with her.

'Do you often just sit in the car?' she said. 'You look as if you do.'

'Like the Thermos mob on the front?' he said. 'Yes, I suppose I do. It passes the time. Lois didn't lose things. A place for everything. She had rules.'

'You didn't stick to them,' Jo said.

'Nothing from the shop out on the pavement. That would have been like taking your clothes off in the street. She was right. You get the stuff outside, it looks pretty rough.'

About a month ago, it must have been, on an evening like this, they had moved three chairs into the sun and set out a trestle table with the items of junk which could stand light falling on them. They had sat there, the three of them, watching the world go by. Well, cars anyway and dogs. Annie had swept the pavement with the broom. She liked doing that. They hadn't sold anything. Trevor would probably remember it too, but he wouldn't mention it. He'd think she was brassed-off enough.

'Did you see Ella on Thursday evening?' she said.

'Yes,' he said. 'Did she tell you? We went for a nice walk. I was flattered she was prepared to put up with me. Boring old fellow like me.'

'I don't suppose you happened to notice Felpo's van anywhere nearby, did you?' she said. It seemed the simplest way to ask directly.

He looked puzzled. 'No, but that doesn't mean it wasn't there,' he said.

He started to tell her about someone called Frankie, but Jo was barely listening. She was telling herself that if Felpo had known Ella had lied, he would have stayed. She recognised it as one of those bargains made between two fools. Hope based on an alternative in the past, which hadn't happened. Sweet nothing. Ella's idea of reparation was to cause trouble – then to carry on living. It had to do with her age. She'd done what she could. She remembered Ella standing against the window in the kitchen. She supposed someone might mistake them for each other from the back.

'I got the stuff from Ena Tiemann,' Trevor said. 'It's in boxes in the back. She's breaking out. Decided to part with all the heirlooms she wrapped up and put away when her mother died. She says she needs the space.'

'What for?' Jo said.

'I didn't ask her. They do that sometimes. Clear the decks. The only freedom left, turning out a cupboard,' he said.

'Let's not think about it,' she said.

'She bought a new blouse too. Swallowed the spare buttons. Said she remembered thinking they looked like little white pills in their nice plastic packet and the next thing she knew she'd taken them with water.'

'Was that before or after she turned the cupboard out?' Jo said.

'Before, I think.'

'I might try it,' Jo said.

'September tomorrow,' Trevor said.

'Yes,' Jo said. 'It is.'

She thought of Ena Tiemann sitting in her chair waiting for the carer to arrive to put her to bed. She wouldn't know what she was waiting for, nor, for the time being, where she was. From the clouds of her mind, household items would emerge – plates with green and gold rims, a dish in the shape of a lettuce leaf, a fruit bowl with blue dragons chasing round it, a photograph of a girl dressed up as a princess, waving at the camera. She wouldn't know why she was thinking of them.

'We could see what's in the box,' Trevor said. 'Shall we? It's all in newspaper. Find out the weather forecast forty years ago.'

'All right,' she said.

A woman came round the side of the coastguard station and steadied herself on the near wall. She had been running, for exercise, and was catching her breath. Her eyes, over-focused by exertion, fixed on them. Jo knew that the woman wasn't actually seeing, but she was relieved that they hadn't already got out in the open and started unwrapping the Apostle spoons. Although the windows on either side of the car were open, she was hidden by the reflections on the chalky glass to the front.